great!

Please, Rebecca prayed. Let this be the right thing for my son....

She stood in the doorway, clutching her robe to her, and watched Tucker walk briskly to a sedan parked across the street.

There had been a time when she would have sworn Tucker Malloy didn't feel anything at all. But when she saw him fold his arms across the steering wheel and then rest his forehead against them, she had to admit that the man was feeling something very strongly tonight.

It seemed he knew exactly what he'd missed by being away all these years.

Then Rebecca found tears falling freely down her face, as she suspected they were falling down his.

And she slid down to sit on the front steps and cried as she hadn't in years—cried for herself, for him, for their son and for all the days gone by....

Dear Reader,

As always, it's difficult to know where to begin when talking about this month's Intimate Moments lineup. We've got so many wonderful books and authors that I guess the only place to start is at the beginning, with Kathleen Creighton's American Hero title, *A Wanted Man.* And I promise you'll want Mike Lanagan for yourself once you start reading this exciting story about reporter-on-the-run Mike and farmer Lucy Brown, the woman who thinks he's just a drifter but takes him in anyway. Like Lucy, you'll take him right into your heart and never let him go.

In *No Easy Way Out,* Paula Detmer Riggs gives us a hero with a dark secret and a heroine with a long memory. *Days Gone By* is the newest from Sally Tyler Hayes, a second-chance story with an irresistible six-year-old in the middle. Kim Cates makes her first appearance in the line with *Uncertain Angels,* the story of a right-side-of-the-tracks woman who finds herself challenged by a do-gooder in black leather. In *For the Love of a Child,* Catherine Palmer brings together a once-married couple and the voiceless boy whom heroine Lilia Eden hopes to adopt. When little Colin finally speaks, you'll have tears in your eyes. Finally, there's *Rancher's Choice,* by Kylie Brant, whom you met as our 1992 Premiere author. I think you'll agree that this book is a fitting follow-up to her smashing debut.

Enjoy!

Leslie Wainger
Senior Editor and Editorial Coordinator

Please address questions and book requests to:
Reader Service
U.S.: P.O. Box 1325, Buffalo, NY 14269
Canadian: P.O. Box 1050, Niagara Falls, Ont. L2E 7G7

DAYS GONE BY

Sally
Tyler
Hayes

Silhouette®
INTIMATE MOMENTS®
Published by Silhouette Books New York
America's Publisher of Contemporary Romance

SILHOUETTE BOOKS

ISBN 0-373-07549-9

DAYS GONE BY

Books by Sally Tyler Hayes

Silhouette Intimate Moments

Whose Child Is This? #439
Dixon's Bluff #485
Days Gone By #549

SALLY TYLER HAYES

lives by the ocean—a long-held dream of hers—with her husband, her young son and new baby daughter. A journalist for a newspaper in her home state of South Carolina, she fondly remembers that her decision to write and explore the frontiers of romance came at about the same time she discovered, in junior high, that she'd never be able to join the crew of the *Starship Enterprise*.

Busy with a full-time job and a full-time family, she confesses that she writes during her children's nap time and after they go to bed at night.

To Laura Jane,
my bright-eyed,
sugar-sweet girl

Chapter 1

The letter—a bizarre form of self-torture wrapped in the finest cream-colored stationery—was halfway across the room, yet the distance didn't diminish the power it held over him.

In the darkened office, leaning back in the big leather chair and facing the windows, Tucker Malloy noticed with dismay that the heavy crystal glass in his hand was empty once again. And he was still sober—at least enough to know that he didn't want to open the damned letter. It had a power over him, more power than the half-empty little bottle of Jack Daniels he'd chosen to abuse his body with tonight.

This was the ninth letter he'd received, and each one seemed harder to bear than the previous one. This one burned him, like the flames of an icy-cold fire, hotter than the unadulterated whiskey sliding down his throat.

It was Black Label stock—the good stuff.

Black Jack, he recalled with a smile as he looked out the window again, watching the trails of cars that ran thick up and down the highway.

He'd discovered the whiskey buried in a desk drawer. Must have been a present, because he didn't buy the stuff anymore. And when he had been buying it, he never would have picked up a bottle this small.

Not that he had a drinking problem. He'd just gotten worried about four years ago—no, *exactly* four years ago, when the first letter had arrived—that it would be too easy, given his state of mind at the time, for him to develop a drinking problem. He'd come to look forward, a little too much, to that first drink of the evening.

That was the summer he quit drinking, just to be on the safe side.

It was the summer when he decided he didn't like what he'd made of his life. The summer when he realized he didn't like himself that much. The summer when he'd acknowledged for the first time that he couldn't run away from his past nearly as easily as he'd first thought.

And now? Here he was in a cold sweat in the air-conditioned room, just considering the idea that he'd made a monumental mistake all those years ago, wondering what it would take to put it all to right.

If it could ever be right again.

One more drink, he told himself. It was that time of year, after all, one of the two days a year when he let himself have a drink.

It was June. A too-hot Thursday in June. Deliberately, he didn't know the date.

The appointment calendar that usually sat in the upper-left corner of his desk was buried somewhere in a drawer. In June, he depended on Jeanie, his secretary, to keep him up-to-date on his appointments, delineated only by day of the week. Dates weren't all that necessary, he had found.

On July 1—Jeanie would tell him the date—he'd pull out his calendar again.

It must be close to that now, because the letter had arrived. That meant the birthday had passed, and the picture in the letter had most likely been taken on Sammy's birthday.

He wasn't sure, of course, because he hadn't opened the letter. Not this one. Or the one that arrived shortly after Christmas. Or the one that came the previous June. Or any of the others.

Only the first one—the one that arrived four years ago—had been opened, then carefully sealed again. He didn't need to see the picture. He carried the image in his mind as clearly as if it had been yesterday.

He had eight of those letters at home in the bottom of a drawer he never opened. This one on the shelf, the one that had come today, made nine.

Nine letters, he thought as he emptied the glass and tipped the little bottle again. Six years had come and gone.

And a son he wouldn't know if they brushed past each other on the sidewalk.

Tucker started drinking around four on Thursday, soon after the state office building closed for the weekend. He downed the little bottle by five and made it home thirty minutes later in a taxi.

He lost another two hours staring at the picture, then at all the pictures. He opened all the letters, one by one, starting with the one from Sammy's second birthday and ending with this one, from his sixth birthday on June 18.

There they were, Sammy with Rebecca—looking even more beautiful than the woman he'd married so long ago—then Sammy, Rebecca and her husband, Brian Sandelle, huddled together so that they all fit in the picture. One big, happy family—a little boy, his mother and a substitute father. That's what he'd wanted them all to be, a real family. There was no room for him there.

He'd been sure when Rebecca divorced him that she and Brian would marry, that Sammy would find a father in the man. Tucker, for reasons that were both selfish and selfless, had wanted Sammy to have a good father. He'd been honest enough with himself to know that he wouldn't be a good father for Sammy and that he and Rebecca probably weren't going to stay together.

Tucker had loved Rebecca as best he could, loved her enough to want her to be happy. And he knew he would never make her happy. The knowledge had helped him to step back and give Brian, her childhood sweetheart, another chance with her.

And there were his selfish reasons, as well. He wasn't cut out to be a married man, much less a father. Despite his misgivings about his own ability to be a good husband, he'd married Rebecca, because she was a marrying kind of woman, and he'd been willing to do anything to make her his.

And when the time had come, when the relationship had soured and they'd hurt each other more than he'd believed possible, along came Sammy.

The baby had scared Tucker to death and sent him searching for a way out. Right on cue came Brian Sandelle, and before long, Tucker saw a way to ease his guilty conscience.

After all, Tucker couldn't be such a rotten guy if Rebecca and Sammy found a way to be happier with Brian than they ever would have been with him. At least that's what he'd told himself.

He'd seen the three of them together—Sammy, Rebecca and Brian—in that first picture he'd received, the one taken at Sammy's second birthday. He should be happy for them, he told himself. But he still had to grit his teeth to keep from groaning at the thought of Rebecca with another man. And now he was wondering what kind of father Brian Sandelle had made for Sammy and whether there was any room in the boy's life for him.

Tucker sat there and stared at the pictures spread out before him. It hurt as much as he thought it would, more than the whiskey could mask, to see with his own eyes the passing of time. Time he'd missed. All the days gone by, days he could never get back. Days his son used to grow into a person he didn't know at all, to grow without the father he probably didn't even remember.

But the thing that hurt most of all was the look in the little boy's eyes in the most recent picture. There was a smile on his lips, but none in his eyes.

Why did his little boy have such sad eyes? he wondered as he fumbled with the phone, then stopped short when he realized he didn't know the number to dial.

That was good, he realized. He wasn't ready to call just yet. He needed another minute to collect himself.

Something deep within him—his heart, maybe his soul—had shattered like a broken glass when he'd seen the look in those big brown eyes.

I did it for you, Sammy.

He'd told himself that for five years, but it didn't wash anymore. He couldn't deny the blood ties that linked him and this sad little sandy-haired boy. Tucker needed him, with a need deeper than any he'd ever known, a need that had grown with each day it had been denied.

He both hoped and feared that the little boy still needed him, as well. Hoped because he wanted desperately to have another chance with him. Feared because that meant the boy had needed Tucker in the past, but he hadn't been there. Feared because he might not be able to make that up to Sammy.

Tucker stared at the clock. It was seven-thirty here, so that made it eight-thirty in Florida.

He didn't even know where his own son was living. He sent child-support payments regularly, but at Rebecca's request, they went to her lawyer, who forwarded them to her.

She hadn't wanted anything to do with Tucker after the divorce, and he couldn't blame her for that.

Would she put up with him now if Sammy agreed to see him after all this time?

Tucker picked up the phone. Quickly, before he could change his mind, he dialed information.

"In Tallahassee," he told the operator. "Brian or Rebecca Sandelle?"

"I'm sorry, sir. Checking Tallahassee . . . I don't have a Brian or Rebecca Sandelle."

"Thank you," he said and sat there for who knows how long with nothing but the dial tone humming in his ear.

They must have moved.

Only seven-thirty here, eight-thirty there, on a Thursday night. Rebecca's mother, Margaret Harwell, might be home. She'd have the number, and she'd be more than happy to give it to him. Margaret always tried to tell Tucker things he didn't want to hear about the son he never saw. He couldn't bear to hear it, but he hadn't been able to say no when she offered to send the pictures twice a year.

He dialed. "Margaret? This is Tucker. I need a favor."

"Of course, dear. What can I do?"

"Rebecca's phone number."

He heard a choking sound, a half laugh, half cry. "Oh, Tucker. I'm so glad."

"I..." The nerves were getting to him, and his voice was harsher than it should have been. "Oh, God, Margaret."

"He needs you, Tucker. They both do. You need them, too."

She gave him a Tallahassee number, and he wrote it down with a shaky hand.

He said goodbye quickly, hung up the phone once more and let his eyes wander around the bland little room. A rumpled tan sofa, a coffee table, a television and a bookshelf. Nothing else. He kept the place empty, like his life was these days.

His eyes went back to the coffee table, to the bottle sitting there. No more Black Jack. There hadn't been enough there to make him much more than tipsy, and that had been hours ago.

Nothing but him and the phone, the number and a little boy with sad brown eyes.

Tucker swallowed hard and lifted the receiver as he wondered what sort of reception he'd receive at the other end from Rebecca.

Did she still hate him? She had a right. Would she try to keep him away from their son? He hoped not. He didn't want to fight with her anymore.

He fumbled the number the first time, had to hang up and dial again.

Damn! he muttered as he dialed again and the phone started to ring.

"Hello."

Oh, damn! It wasn't Rebecca. Why had he been so sure Rebecca would answer the phone?

"Hello?" The voice on the other end was quiet and small. A little boy's voice.

Tucker nearly dropped the phone. He opened his mouth twice before he got any sound out.

"Sammy?"

"Yes."

So small, so easily hurt. What had he done?

"Sammy, this is—" He didn't know what to say. God, that hurt. A six-year-old wouldn't remember someone he last saw when he was only a few months old. And whether Sammy knew about him or not, he sure wouldn't know Tucker as his dad.

"Sammy, this is . . . Tucker."

Nothing but silence came across the line.

Tucker was sure he felt his heart crack open inside his chest. He wasn't sure he could go on, but now that he'd started, he couldn't hang up on the boy.

"Sammy? Is your mother there?"

"Uh-huh."

So little, surely so confused, so fragile.

The picture, now lying on the table, was still clear in Tucker's mind. The bright candles on the cake, six of them for the years and one to grow on, the smile on the boy's lips that didn't reach his eyes. Sad brown eyes. How could a little boy looking at his birthday cake seem so sad?

"Could you go get your mom for me, Sammy?"

"Uh-huh."

And he heard it then, heard that sadness in the timid little voice, heard it shoot across the miles that separated them, across the years, until it practically shouted at him.

Fool, his conscience taunted him. You had it all, and you threw it away.

He heard a little sob come across the line, then another, felt tears pool in his own eyes and run down his face, one after another. He would have bet money he didn't know how to cry anymore.

All this time . . . what had he done?

"Sammy?" He choked on the name.

"Uh-huh."

"Your mom?"

"Okay . . . Tucker?" Neither one of them breathed. "Tucker . . . my dad?"

Feelings he'd denied for so long, he'd buried so deep in his soul, came bubbling up inside him, and he was sure he was going to choke.

At some point in the conversation, Tucker had gotten to his feet and started to pace. But now, as that innocent question reached him, his legs simply gave out beneath him and he sat down hard on the worse-for-wear tweed sofa.

"Tucker . . . my dad?"

He heard it again and again, a little sob coming so clearly through the telephone he was holding so tight, he wouldn't be surprised if it snapped in two in his hands.

"Yes, Sammy. I'm your dad."

The little boy didn't say anything else. Once more Tucker heard a sob, then a sniffle, a swish that he suspected was a little hand being pulled impatiently past a runny nose, then a clatter that must have been the telephone receiver banging against something.

A door opened in the background; then his little boy started to yell.

"Mommy!"

* * *

"Sammy? We're out here on the deck," Rebecca called.

"Mommy!"

The distress was much stronger then, much more than that of a little boy looking for his mother. She jumped up and met him at the French doors. Kneeling down on one knee in front of him, she saw the tear-stained face, saw the frightened eyes, the trembling lower lip.

Rebecca pulled him close and squeezed him to her. "Oh, baby. What's the matter?"

"Not a baby." The protest was muffled against her shirt.

"Of course not." She smiled as she whispered against sweet-smelling, sandy-blond hair.

She should have known better than to call him that. There was a seven-year-old know-it-all at the soccer field named Jimmy Horton who made fun of Sammy last week when Sammy got upset about missing one-too-many balls that came his way.

Jimmy Horton must have been the one who told Sammy that big boys didn't cry, because now he worried about that as well as the missed balls. Sammy was always worried about something.

She kissed the top of his head and squeezed him again. "Now, what's the trouble?"

Rebecca tried to pull away from him so she could see his face, but Sammy's skinny little arms held on for all he was worth and he nuzzled against her.

"Man on the phone," he whimpered.

She saw now that the receiver was lying on top of the table.

"What did he say to you, Sammy?"

"My dad."

"What?" Rebecca was sure she hadn't heard him correctly. Very carefully, very deliberately, she untangled herself from the skinny little arms and pushed him far enough away so she could look him in the eye and hear him clearly. "Who's on the telephone?"

Sammy sniffled once more, raked the back of one hand across his eyes, eyes that shimmered with even more tears and made him look as if his heart had broken. "He says he's my dad."

Surely not, Rebecca thought. Definitely not. So much time had gone by, and the break had been so complete.

When Tucker Malloy was done with a woman, he was done. He didn't look back. He didn't try to hang on, even if the woman was the mother of his child.

Yet she eyed the telephone suspiciously now, almost fearfully. She didn't understand exactly what had gone wrong in their brief marriage—she'd long since given up trying to understand what went wrong. She no longer played that cruel game of what ifs. What if she'd been older, stronger, sexier, more sure of herself, more honest with him?

And as for the way the man had managed so successfully to cut himself out of their son's life? She'd wrestled with that for so long, she didn't even allow herself to get mad about it anymore.

The anger was too strong, too destructive. If she allowed herself to dwell on that emotion, it would consume her very being. And she wasn't about to let Tucker have that kind of power over her.

"Sammy, why don't you go outside with Brian. He's about to light the grill and start the burgers, Okay?"

He must have agreed, because she heard his footsteps as he went outside, then heard the door close behind him. She hadn't looked up when she spoke. She was staring at the telephone receiver and its tan cord in the same way she'd eye a snake in the grass.

Surely not, she thought, yet she still braced herself as she picked up the telephone. "Who is this?"

"Rebecca?"

Oh, dear Lord. She'd never forget that voice, never forget the pain they had brought to each other. A half-dozen years ago she would have done anything to hang on to that man. Now she simply wanted to be left alone.

"What do you want, Tucker? And what in God's name did you say to my son?"

"I'm sorry." She heard a long, heavy sigh. "I didn't mean to upset him."

Rebecca laughed coldly at the very idea. "Upset him? It's been nearly six years without so much as a peep out of you, Tucker."

He didn't say anything, and Rebecca laughed again. "He doesn't even know you, nothing but your name. As far as he's concerned, he doesn't even have a father. And after all this time, you think you can just pick up the phone and say, 'Hi. You may not remember me, but this is your father'?"

"It wasn't . . . Rebecca, I just didn't expect him to answer the phone."

"He's six years old now. He answers the phone. He takes out the garbage. He cleans up his own room. He plays soccer. He does all sorts of things you wouldn't begin to imagine."

She felt the rage then, the heated anger that she'd denied for so long. She hadn't escaped it, merely pushed it down deep inside her, and now it all threatened to come bursting out like fiery lava from a volcano. She was seething.

"Rebecca?" Brian was standing in the doorway, watching her carefully, and she knew what he saw—an angry, frightened, out-of-control woman. A few seconds on the phone with Tucker, and he'd reduced her to this. He was poison. Pure poison.

She put her hand over the mouthpiece of the phone to muffle the sound and looked at the man in front of her.

Brian stood there, tall, dark and handsome... open, honest and loving. Legions of women would have no trouble loving Brian Sandelle. He was dependable, successful and steady as a rock. She'd known him her whole life, and he'd never let her down.

So what was missing in their relationship? What else could she possibly want from him? How long would she keep comparing him to Tucker Malloy? And how long—for a reason that was totally incomprehensible to her even after all these years—would Brian be judged and found wanting?

She wondered if he knew it, too. And she wondered how much longer he was going to put up with it.

"I'm all right, Brian." He obviously didn't buy that, but when he took a step forward, she put up a hand to hold him off. "Please, just take care of Sammy for me, and I'll be there in a minute."

Silent and shaken, she stood there and watched him go before she turned her attention back to the phone.

"What do you want, Tucker?"

"Sammy." His voice was low and gruff, the words muffled—by the miles, she decided. It couldn't be his emotions getting the best of him, because she'd decided long ago that Tucker didn't feel anything—at least not for long. "I want to see Sammy."

"Oh?" Maybe she was more vindictive than she thought, because more than anything she wanted to hurt

Tucker as much as she possibly could. "And then you can disappear for another six years and leave me to explain that to him as well, right? Damn you, Tucker. What makes you think he wants to see you, anyway?"

Tears. Dammit, those were tears running down her face, choking her up inside so she could barely speak.

"Just once, Rebecca. Let me see him just once, and if he doesn't ever want to see me again, he won't have to. I'll disappear again. I swear."

"I'm sure disappearing wouldn't be any problem for you. But what if he doesn't want you to? What if he wants you to stay, Tucker? What if he comes to depend upon you, to look forward to seeing you every now and then, and you can't handle that? What do I say to him when you break his little heart all over again?"

She clamped her hand over the mouthpiece and hoped it would muffle the sob that followed her angry, shaky words.

They were silent for a moment, yet both of them were aware of the other on the end of the line.

"Just once, Rebecca."

If she didn't know better, she would have sworn he was begging. But Tucker Malloy didn't beg for anything. He took what he wanted, and he was so smooth that the person doing the giving didn't even think to resist. And when he'd taken his fill, he was gone.

"Rebecca? I don't want to hurt him. I just want to see him. I have to."

"Damn you!" She cursed him again, then tried to rein in the hysteria that was threatening to overtake her. "You've already hurt him more than you'll ever know."

"Once. Just once. And I won't ask again." He waited. "Will you ask him? Or should I?"

So like him, she thought. Assume that the other person would accept his wishes and roll on from there. And never, ever, give up until he was damned good and ready to do so.

Dear Lord, she wished she could tell him to go to the devil, wished she could tell him truthfully that her son was doing just fine without Tucker and didn't care that his own father had shown up now after six years of silence.

But she couldn't. As much as it frightened her to think of the damage Tucker could do, to think of how fragile Sammy was right now where his father was concerned, she couldn't deny that her baby boy needed his father very much.

"I'll think about it," she whispered fiercely. "But, Tucker, I'm warning you. I'm not the mousy little girl you walked away from all those years ago. You hurt him any more than you already have, and I swear you'll pay."

Chapter 2

Rebecca slammed down the phone. She stood by the countertop, trembling and hurting while her stomach turned on itself and started that slow burn that she knew so well.

So long ago, before she'd left Tucker, she'd lived with this constant ache in her midsection. She'd literally made herself sick over that man.

How dare he come back after all this time?

"I guess I don't have to ask if that really was Tucker on the phone?"

Brian caught her standing there, leaning back against the counter with her arms wrapped around her middle.

Rebecca dropped her arms and considered begging for just a little time alone in some dark, quiet place before she had to go over this with Brian. But the look on his face told her she wouldn't have the luxury of that time alone.

"What the hell did he want?" Brian barked.

She jumped at the harsh tone—his Tucker voice, Rebecca thought. Her rational, levelheaded Brian saw red every time the name Tucker Malloy came up. And whether the name was ever actually spoken or not, Tucker seemed to be forever wedged between them.

"He wants to see Sammy," she said quietly.

"Oh? He actually remembered the boy's name? Or did you have to remind him?"

"Brian." Rebecca started to pray then.

She prayed for strength, for patience and mostly for understanding. And when understanding proved to be impossible to come by, she prayed that she'd simply be able to accept all that had happened and put it behind her. "Please. Just give me a minute."

"Hell, Rebecca, he doesn't deserve a minute of your time. He wrote off you and that little boy years ago. You're not actually going to let him see Sammy, are you?"

"I don't know."

"Well, I don't know how you can even consider it."

Amazing, Rebecca thought as she watched Brian seething and shouting, so near to completely losing control. It was amazing what Tucker could still do to them both.

"Brian, I haven't so much as considered it yet. I just got off the phone, and I'm still trying to make myself believe that he even called me after all this time."

"But you are considering letting him see Sammy."

"Yes. I am."

"God, Rebecca." Brian shook his head back and forth. "How can you even think about it?"

Her arms went back around her midsection, and the old familiar ache flared up again. "How can I not think about it. You know what's going on with Sammy. He needs a father now.''

Brian grabbed her in an urgent hold. "He needs me. *Me.* Not somebody who's just going to break his heart all over again. The boy needs me."

He was hurting her then with his painful grip, but she suspected that of the two of them, he was hurting more than she was. "I'm sorry, Brian."

And she was sorry, for all that they'd wanted from each other, for all the years they'd loved each other and still never gotten their relationship quite right.

Brian shook her a little as he swore. "Dammit, I'm more of a father to that little boy already than Tucker Malloy ever was. I should have become his father long ago. And it's long past the time when I should have become your husband."

He should have. She closed her eyes against the pain she saw in his face. She loved Brian Sandelle. It seemed like she had forever. She still did, yet she couldn't bring herself to become his wife.

"I'm sorry, Brian," she said, apologizing for so much more than Tucker's phone call.

She was sorry that they'd never been able to let go of each other, despite all the frustration and pain it had caused them both. But the time was coming to admit that, she realized, and wondered if he realized it, too. Time was coming when they had to face up to the fact that it would never be right between them, that they couldn't keep trying to make it so.

"Rebecca? Are you—" He was watching her so closely now, and he must have seen the gut-deep sadness in her eyes as she started the conversation they'd been avoiding for so long.

Her eyes felt so thick and heavy, as they filled with tears. Her heart was filled with dread. She loved Brian dearly, and she didn't want to hurt him anymore.

Rebecca cupped her hand to his cheek, looked deep into his eyes and shook her head sadly. "I'm so sorry."

He paused then, while the fury filled his stormy eyes. Brian turned his back to her, then leaned into the counter with his hands on either side of him, his head hanging low.

"So am I," he said as he looked down at the counter. "I'm tired of waiting for you to get over him. And I'm damned sure sick of having your ex-husband's ghost in the bed between us."

Rebecca couldn't help but flinch at that. She didn't want Tucker there any more than Brian did, but she hadn't figured out how to get him out. Although she suspected the problem now was that none of them had been to bed together in months.

Rebecca had been avoiding Brian, making excuses to him, doing whatever she could to avoid that particular aspect of their relationship. It wasn't that she had a lot of hang-ups about sex or that Brian wasn't a kind, considerate, patient lover.

He just wasn't... *Tucker Malloy.*

Rebecca winced at the very thought running through her own head. She didn't want Tucker in her bed any more than she wanted him in her life. She just wanted some of those feelings back. She wanted to find them with someone else.

Making love to Tucker was a monumental thing, an overwhelming, scalding, all-engulfing thing. There was such a power that ran between them, a passion, a need so strong, that it both fascinated and frightened her; a power she feared she'd never find with anyone else. It was a feeling she hadn't found with Brian.

"Brian—" She'd forgotten for a minute that she was still keeping him waiting.

"Don't." He turned and quieted her with a finger against her lips and the pain in his eyes. "I've done everything I know to do, Rebecca. I can't compete with the man's ghost. But maybe, just maybe now that he's back, maybe once he rips your heart out again, you'll remember him for what he is and not for what you wanted him to be. Maybe then you'll see that he'll never be able to make you happy."

She knew that, Rebecca protested to herself. She knew that Tucker was never going to make her happy, just as she knew she couldn't marry Brian. In some intangible way, their relationship just wasn't right. She wondered if it would ever be right.

"One more thing," he said as he gathered his keys and his sunglasses from the counter. "The paper mill—some company bought the property, and it looks like they're going to try to resurrect the whole thing."

For the second time that night, Rebecca felt as if a stiff breeze could have knocked her flat. She was as surprised as she'd been when she heard Tucker's voice coming through the telephone. "Can . . . can they do that?" she managed to say.

"Maybe."

He pocketed the keys with a nonchalance that irritated her now, because he knew very well how much this news would upset her. He also knew how bitterly she and Tucker had fought over that project six years ago.

"Can we stop them?"

"Maybe." Brian slid the sunglasses into place.

"Can we?"

He shrugged, frowned, then admitted, "Maybe. Maybe not. It's a tough call. Got a better chance if you're steering the ship."

"Oh, no." She had enough of her wits about her to be quick with that answer. "I can't handle it right now, Brian. I'm way behind on the Arts Center fund-raiser, and I have three big jobs lined up behind it."

Rebecca made a living out of finding other people money. The homeless shelter, the AIDS clinic, the Arts Center, she'd worked for them all. People who needed to raise money in Tallahassee, whatever the cause, called on Rebecca.

"I can't do it," she repeated, knowing what she was really saying was that she didn't *want* to do it. It would bring up too many unhappy memories for her, and she had about as many as she could handle coming at her already with just a phone call from Tucker.

"Just give it some thought, honey," Brian urged. "We're getting our coalition back together, and we need you. Nobody was more upset than you were at the thought of the mill ruining that gorgeous river and the park just downstream."

Or at the thought of her husband being the one to get PaperWorks Inc. the permits it needed to do that to the river, she thought. And it hadn't meant a thing to Tucker, nothing but a job to do and more money to make.

A few months after they'd separated, Paperworks Inc. was sold, and the new owners dropped their plans to build the paper mill. But now it was all starting again.

"I just can't do it, Brian. Tell them if they need money, and I'm sure they will, I'll do everything I can to get it for them. But I can't head up the whole project."

"I'll tell them you're thinking about it, okay?"

Rebecca couldn't argue with him now. She simply didn't have the strength for it. "Okay, I will. And about everything else, I'm—"

He held up his hands as if to hold back her words, then leaned over and kissed her lightly on the lips. "Get over him, Rebecca. Call me when you do, and I'll be there. God help me, I'll probably always be there for you."

Then he turned and left.

Rebecca looked at the clock on the kitchen wall and shook her head in wonder. The paper mill project again and Tucker, all in the same day. No more than an hour had passed since her ex-husband had called, yet it felt as if she'd lived through years—years she didn't care to recall.

And now came the truly hard part—she had to face her son and try to explain this to him.

Sammy wasn't in the house. He wasn't on the back deck. And she didn't see him in the backyard.

Then she heard an ominous *ping,* like the noise a rock makes when it's thrown into a pool of water.

She raced for the hedge that separated her yard from Mr. Bennett's. There was a little gap in the hedge near the back corner of the yard. As she reached the gap, she could see Sammy joylessly pitching pebbles into Mr. Bennett's goldfish pond.

Shock held her motionless for a long moment. Sammy had never, ever, crossed through the hedge and gone near that damned pond.

Most children found the temptation of being able to throw a rock into a pool of water too much to deny. And it was even more irresistible because it made Mr. Bennett crazy. He had a hissy fit whenever he caught any child in his yard, much less near that silly pond with the oversize colored fish.

The old man had decorated the bottom of the little artificial pond with special lights and pretty colored stones. The plain old pebbles the children threw in there destroyed the ambience of the pool, he explained endlessly to anyone foolish enough to be caught nearby when there was trouble with the pond. Rebecca didn't want any more trouble tonight.

Sammy knew how obsessed the old man was with the pond. He knew never to go near the place. And although he may have been tempted before, he was simply too timid to take the risk.

Her little boy was like that—a little too shy, too easily hurt. He was a lot like Rebecca had been as a child.

But the little boy standing in plain sight of the Bennett house and calmly throwing pebbles into the pond wasn't timid. He was mad.

Her little boy was so full of anger these days. And seeing her child hurt like this hurt Rebecca more than anything that had happened tonight.

She could stand anything, except seeing her son hurt.

"Sammy!" she said urgently but softly from her place in the hole in the hedge.

The little boy didn't acknowledge the call.

"Sammy, please?"

Nothing. Rebecca glanced up at the lighted windows of the Bennett house and was relieved to see no one through the glass. She sprinted across the yard to Sammy's side, grabbed his hand and turned to run back the other way. But Sammy didn't budge. It was like pulling on deadweight.

"Sammy, come on." She got down on her knees in front of him and turned him to face her so they were eye to eye. Eye to tear-filled brown eye.

"No!" He tried to pull out of her hold, but she wouldn't let him.

Rebecca watched him and wondered how anyone so small could be filled with so much sadness, covered up by so much anger. "What is it, baby?"

"I'm not a baby!" he said fiercely.

Rebecca closed her eyes and counted to ten. She knew better than to call him that, especially when he was upset. "I know, Sammy. Can we go home now?"

He just stood there, small and miserable in the fading light, a sight that broke her heart all over again.

Rebecca took his hand and loosened his fierce hold on the pebbles. They both stared down at the smooth stones.

Sammy sniffled once, then again, before hesitantly lifting his eyes to hers. "Why didn't he wanna talk to me?"

"You mean . . . your dad?"

With a trembling lower lip and a runny nose, he nodded.

"Oh, Sammy? Is that what this is all about?"

He swiped the back of his hand past his runny nose, then nodded.

"It was him. I know it was," Sammy rushed on breathlessly. "He said his name was Tucker, but I know it was my dad 'cause you told me that was his name. So I asked him if he was my dad, and he said he was. And then he didn't even wanna talk to me. He just wanted you."

"Sammy," Rebecca said, closing her eyes and making her decision right then. And she prayed that she was doing the right thing. She had to do the right thing for her little boy. "Your dad doesn't just want to talk to you on the phone. He wants to come see you."

Those shimmering brown eyes flew up to her face, and Rebecca saw the tears caught in his incredibly long, thick eyelashes. Oh, she remembered those eyes. Sometimes he was so like Tucker that the sight of Sammy stole the breath from her lungs. It was so hard to get over Tucker when the most precious thing in her world was a miniature version of him.

She brushed Sammy's tears away for him.

"He's coming here?" Sammy looked stunned.

"Yes." She smiled, despite her misgivings.

"Really?"

"Yes."

"Wow!" He gave her a trembling smile. "And I can show him my room and my train set, and take him to soccer practice and to meet Jimmy Horton and his dad?"

"Yes." If she had to drag the man by the hair on his head, Tucker would go. And he'd be suitably impressed with it all.

"Wow!" Sammy yelled as he jumped for joy, then headed for the hole in the hedge. "Come on, Mom. We gotta get outta here before Mr. Bennett catches us."

And that settled that, Rebecca decided as she stood up and dusted off her pants. Tucker Malloy was going to get a chance to see his son.

Chapter 3

The phone was ringing, and Rebecca was on her way to answer it when the doorbell sounded.

She paused, trapped between the two sounds, while she wondered whether she could get away with ignoring them both.

She was tired, drained actually, in the little more than twenty-four hours since Tucker called, and she expected little, if any, rest tonight. Tomorrow, she expected, would be even worse.

Tomorrow, Tucker was coming to see his son.

Sammy was too excited to sleep.

Rebecca was too terrified.

She'd just turned out the light and closed the door to her little boy's room, she hoped for the final time tonight.

On her way to the couch, where she planned to collapse and brood about what lay ahead of her, the phone rang.

Probably Brian. The thought made her pause before answering. They'd already had one fight via telephone earlier this evening. She wasn't up to another. She had only mere hours left in which to prepare herself to face her ex-husband. She didn't need to listen to Brian tell her what a mistake she was making by allowing the meeting to take place.

Rebecca was relieved when the doorbell rang. It saved her, at least for a moment, from deciding whether to answer the telephone at all.

The barrier of the heavy wooden door swung past, bringing a blast of humid night air with it. The heat, relentless in its assault on the city in June, ran over her like a steamroller, but it was nothing compared to the impact of the sight of the man standing before her.

Tucker Malloy, twelve hours ahead of schedule.

And she wasn't ready. She might never have been ready to face him again, but she wished she'd at least had some time to prepare herself. She closed her eyes for a moment, opened them again and found him still standing there in front of her.

She watched him as he waited, still and silent, while she could do nothing but stand there and stare at him. She wondered why the very sight of him had the power to take her world and tilt it alarmingly on its axis, to leave her as unsteady as Southern California after one of the many tremors that rocked the area.

Rebecca meant to be so cool to him, so unaffected. She planned on being dignified and coldly polite. Instead, she was clutching the door, the only solid thing within reach that didn't seem to be swaying back and forth.

She'd made a grave error in thinking that the sight of him after all these years would mean nothing to her. Old wounds came thundering to the surface, anger that had been suppressed too long, hurts that had never been tended.

Cold politeness was more than she could manage over the shock that came on so strong and so sudden that she felt it grip her lungs, like a vise grinding closed around them. She needed air, and none was to be found.

Her eyes were locked on Tucker's. His locked on hers. Neither of them moved. Neither of them breathed.

In the background, the telephone rang again. In some corner of her mind, Rebecca acknowledged the sound but didn't bother to try to decipher its meaning. Her mind was too busy trying to take in the sight of the man standing before her.

So like him to do this to her, she thought absently. He'd thrown her off balance from the first moment she laid eyes on him, and here he was doing it still.

Not fair, she protested as she stood there clinging to the heavy oak door. She let her eyes slowly roam over him once more and acknowledge what she'd already suspected—he was as gorgeous as always.

"Rebecca?"

She blinked, twice, and damned if he wasn't still there. A little older, a little colder, perhaps, but essentially the same man she'd loved and lost all those years ago.

"Yes?" There. She'd done it. She'd managed to speak, after all.

"Your phone's ringing."

So it was.

In a curious daze, she took it all in again: his trim but powerful body, his impeccably cut, tailor-made suit.

Of course Tucker would still be wearing a killer suit at this hour.

Sandy-colored hair that the sun bleached nearly blond in the summer. Thick, parted on one side and feathered back on the other, with nary a hair out of place.

And those eyes, deep brown with dark, curling lashes, such a contrast to that blondish hair.

He had dimples, too. How many grown men had dimples?

And his smile. He had one that could light up a city block, but he hadn't turned it on tonight. She should probably be grateful for small favors, but she couldn't quite summon up that particular emotion right now.

He just stood there in the doorway, locked in the same spell that held her as well.

So she had a little time, time to wonder about the worry lines that marred the corners of his beautiful eyes and the laugh lines that were missing from the corners of his mouth.

Tucker had always known how to laugh, how to make her laugh, too. That was the first thing she'd loved about him—the way he made her laugh.

And then all the laughter had disappeared. She wondered sometimes, when those joyous days seemed so far away, if they had ever existed at all.

The pain in her chest slowly receded. The vise that had gripped her lungs finally relinquished its hold, and she had to fight not to panic and gasp for air.

She hung on to the door and hoped that with its help, her legs could hold her.

"Rebecca?" He broke the silence again. "Your phone's ringing."

And then she remembered, too late, who was likely to be on that phone.

The answering machine in the kitchen clicked on before she could acknowledge his words. She heard her own recorded voice, heard the whir of the advancing tape, then the long, annoying beep.

"Rebecca?" Brian's voice was clearly audible, coming through the machine. "It's nearly ten, and I can't believe you're not home.... Come on, honey. Pick up the phone."

She couldn't. She couldn't move. She just stared from the machine to Tucker—Tucker was standing on her doorstep.

"Look," Brian continued, "I'm sorry about that fight we had, but I can't just stand by and watch you let that man back into your life."

She knew what was coming then, knew what he was going to say. She knew she didn't want to hear it again, just as she knew she'd waited too late to stop him from saying it.

Yet she had to try. She let go of the door and scrambled for the machine now broadcasting Brian's voice.

"It's been six years, Rebecca. He walked away from you, and he never looked back. He walked straight from your bed to Cheryl Atkinson's, and he—"

She wasn't thinking straight, and when she reached the machine and saw the tape rolling, she grabbed for it. There was an ugly screech as she pulled the running tape from the machine. But the words Brian said didn't stop, because they were coming from the machine, not the tape.

She had to stop his voice, Rebecca decided as she stared at the machine.

She'd never had it out with Tucker after that day she walked into his office and found him locked in a clinch with that woman. What was there to say, anyway? Her husband's actions spoke for themselves. By the time she'd finally made it home that night, he'd collected his things and moved in with Cheryl until a few weeks later when he left town.

Tucker didn't need to know how deeply that had hurt her, and she doubted she could have explained it to him even if she'd wanted to. The kind of pain he'd caused her couldn't be explained in words.

It was the kind of hurt that burrowed down into a woman's soul, the kind she carried with her always, no matter how much time had passed. That kind of pain was so strong at first that it left her curled up in a ball, rocking back and forth, weeping when she wasn't screaming about the unfairness of it all.

Her face burned still at the memory, at the strength of the humiliation she'd felt.

Rebecca fumbled with the volume switch on the machine, couldn't remember exactly where it was and ended up knocking the whole damned thing to the floor.

It landed with a crash, ruined for sure, but she didn't care. She'd silenced Brian. Now all she had to deal with was Tucker.

He was standing just inside the doorway watching her, waiting, probably expecting her to fall apart.

She'd fallen apart so often in the course of their brief marriage.

And in that instant, as it all came roaring back to her, she hated him again. Full-blown, unadulterated hate, the kind she'd felt for him in those first few weeks after she'd found him with that woman.

It had hurt like nothing she'd ever known, and she had no intention of going through anything like that again.

Rebecca was gathering her courage to go and deal with him when the phone rang again.

She picked up the receiver for an instant before slamming it down again, just long enough to disconnect the

call. Then she took the receiver off the hook and placed
it on the countertop. The receiver hummed for a moment, then beeped in the silence that hovered around
them.

It was driving her crazy, but she didn't know what else
to do. Tucker was more than she could deal with right
now. She had no intention of trying to handle Brian as
well.

Scared but determined, angry but resigned to the ne-
cessity of dealing with him, she turned back to Tucker,
who waited uneasily just inside the doorway.

"What do you want, Tucker?" She lifted her chin and
looked him square in the eye.

What did he want? At the moment, it was a damned
good question.

He turned, took his time about closing the door and
securing the lock, then faced her again.

He'd come here thinking he knew exactly what he
wanted, what he needed—his son. And now the sight of
her there, so proud and so hurt, had him thinking all over
again about how very much he'd lost.

Tucker didn't stop to question what drove him to her
or to think about how she'd react. He walked across the
room and stopped so close to her that he could see the
gold flecks in her dark green eyes. She had the most incredible eyes.

Rebecca gave a start, swayed back away from him, and
that worried him even more.

He steadied her with one hand on her arm. He meant
to do no more than that, but he couldn't help but feel the
warmth of her flesh as it reached him, even through the
cool, deep green silk robe.

"Are you all right, Rebecca?" She trembled beneath his touch for just a moment, before she snatched her arm away.

"That is no concern of yours."

It shouldn't be, at least not to the man she believed him to be, not to the man he used to be.

But he was different now. She'd probably laugh in his face if he even tried to explain that to her, but he was different now.

He truly didn't want to hurt her any more than he already had, but it seemed he'd done that just by walking back into her life.

And it seemed he wasn't the only one who hadn't put the past to rest.

"Tucker?" she said impatiently.

"Yes?"

"What do you want?"

He paused to reconsider why he'd come here, wondered if he should explain it to her, if she'd ever be able to understand or if she'd even care.

He stood there sweating as he thought of what was ahead of him. Somehow, he hadn't expected it to be this hard. For some reason, he believed the hard part was actually making the decision to see Sammy, and that everything would get easier from there.

It was the right thing to do. He'd felt that from the moment he'd hung up the phone with Rebecca that first night.

Tucker had spent the past six years tearing his life apart, piece by piece. He'd changed everything—his career, his home, his friends, the women who came and went through his life. The changes had helped, but they hadn't made everything right.

Nothing had felt right.

There was an emptiness in him, a vast space deep in his heart, a black, black hole.

He was going to fill it. He had to, because he couldn't seem to live any longer with this feeling that something was missing, some part of him.

It had to be Sammy. He had to be the key, the missing piece. Tucker wondered if the boy felt it, too, wondered if Sammy had a big, empty space in his little heart, as well.

Tucker hoped Sammy didn't, because he hated to think the boy had suffered like this.

But at the same time, Tucker couldn't help but hope that Sammy felt the same way, because he wanted desperately to find a place in his son's heart to call his own. If—if the boy would let him.

"I need to see Sammy," he told the woman he'd probably always think of as his wife.

"I know." She was clearly puzzled. "Tomorrow."

"No, I need to see him tonight."

"He's asleep, Tucker."

"I was counting on that."

Rebecca stared at him, wondering if she was seeing what she thought she was seeing. Tucker was one smooth operator. Cool, confident, outgoing, good-looking, a man who knew what he wanted and how to get it.

Yet he hesitated now. He was fidgeting with his tie, and a moment ago he'd buttoned his sleek, double-breasted suit one minute, then unbuttoned it the next.

"But if Sammy's asleep..." she began.

"Then it won't matter whether I see him or not."

She noticed his hands then—in the pocket, out of the pocket, one in a fist at his side, then another against the wall, the fingers drumming.

Nerves. It had to be, and it wasn't any wonder that it had taken her so long to recognize it in him, because she'd never seen the man nervous before.

And then a terrible thought came to her. "You're not telling me that you just came out here to get one look at him? That you plan to walk in there and take a peek at him tonight, then disappear tomorrow, are you?"

"No." He flung the word at her through clenched teeth, closed his eyes while he took a deep breath. When he looked at her again, she could have sworn she'd hurt him just by suggesting such a thing.

"Then why?"

"For God's sake, Rebecca, it's been six years since I've seen him."

"And another few hours are going to make that much difference to you?"

"Yes."

She jumped, startled by the vehemence behind the word. He was pacing by now and clearly frustrated by the small amount of space in her living room in which to walk.

"Yes," he said, this time softly, as he faced the doorway. "It makes a hell of a lot of difference."

She didn't understand, but she showed him the way upstairs to Sammy's bedroom. She opened the door to the darkened room and walked in, expecting him to follow, but he didn't.

Deathly pale, he waited just outside the doorway.

"Tucker?"

He didn't seem to hear her, so she waited until some of the color came back into his face, until the fidgeting started again, and he didn't look as if he were about to keel over.

He glanced cautiously through the doorway. His eyes darted over to the bed, to the boy sprawled across it on top of the covers, then quickly looked back down at the floor. He just stood there for the longest time, sweating and looking down at the floor.

And then she realized—he was scared to death.

It seemed to take forever before he made his way inside the room. Suddenly Rebecca realized her heart must be beating just as fast as his, and she'd bet that he had this same choking feeling constricting his throat.

She watched him as he stood there by the bed, the man so like the little boy, the boy who reminded her so much of the man.

Tucker didn't move, didn't say a word. He reached out to touch Sammy, but his hand hung there in the air for a moment, until the hesitation passed. Tucker stroked Sammy's hair once, then again, before he picked up one of the boy's hands, which Tucker measured against one of his own.

He was swaying slightly back and forth beside the bed, the tension radiating from him as he continued to stare at the sleeping boy.

She was watching Sammy, too, and wondering what tomorrow would bring. Please, she prayed, let this be the right thing.

And before she could even finish running through her list of worries, Tucker brushed past her, walked out of the room and down the stairs. She had to scramble to keep up with him, and he was out the door and halfway down the walkway before she realized he intended to leave without saying another word.

"Tucker?"

"See you tomorrow."

The words carried over his shoulder and back to her. He didn't look at her. He just walked briskly to a dark gray sedan parked across the street.

Relieved that he was going, yet surprised at the turmoil she'd witnessed in him, Rebecca stood in the doorway, clutching her robe to her. She stepped back, intending to close the door, and if she had moved a split second faster, she would have missed it.

The car wasn't far from a streetlight, and she could make out his silhouette in the car. She saw him bash his fist down hard against the steering wheel, pounding it again and again, and she flinched for him as she imagined the pain it must be causing him.

But Tucker didn't seem to feel it. There was a time when she would have sworn he didn't feel anything at all.

But she had to admit that when she saw him stop pounding on the steering wheel, saw him fold his arms across it and then rest his forehead against those arms, that the man felt something very strongly tonight.

It seemed Tucker knew exactly what he'd missed by being away from Sammy all these years.

And then Rebecca found the tears falling freely down her own face, as she suspected they were falling down his.

She slid down to sit on the front step and cried like she hadn't in years, cried for her, for him, for Sammy and for all the days gone by.

Rebecca dried her cheeks on the back of her hand and sat there on the step, lost somewhere in the distant past.

And she thought of him, thought of things she hadn't let herself remember in years. She thought of the good times, the sweetness of their early days together.

She couldn't help herself. Just the sight of him brought back so much. She made the mistake of closing her eyes for a moment, and in the blackness before her eyes, she saw him. Not the frightened man she'd seen tonight, but the one who'd caught her eye so long ago—that's who she saw. His image was there, as clear as it had been the day she first laid eyes on him.

She'd been in the garden, sipping sherry, bored to tears by one of her father's colleague's talk about torts, wondering what she was going to do with her life. Nothing new about that. She expected to be bored at dinners for her father's lawyer friends. And she was still waiting for that one moment when everything would fall into place for her, when she'd see the path she was meant to take and find a purpose for herself, which, as yet, had proven elusive.

Then she'd glanced across the garden, across the tops of the deep red and the cream-colored roses in full bloom, to the patio.

The boring lawyer droned on, but the sound of his voice just faded away. The buzz of the party faded as well, and there was nothing but Tucker.

He'd turned at that instant to catch her eye as she glanced over the roses. The sun had glinted off his golden hair, and then he'd smiled.

She'd stood there, her gaze locked on his, her thoughts rushing ahead. And in that instant, all things seemed possible for them.

Tucker had been simply stunning. He was one of those truly beautiful men, the slyly wicked smile, the laughing eyes and sunlit hair. A pretty boy, her mother had remarked later that night. No, Rebecca thought, he couldn't be a pretty boy, because he was so unmistakably a man.

Rebecca had been twenty, a terribly young, terribly shy and insecure twenty. Tucker hadn't seemed to notice.

That had been one of the first things she'd loved about him—that his vision of her had been so different from her own.

She'd thought herself quite ordinary. He'd insisted she was beautiful.

And he made her laugh. He was teasing her one minute and tantalizing her the next.

Her father brought a lot of young lawyers home to dinner, but never one who had kicked her heart into high gear with just one look.

Tucker had said all the right things to her father, charmed her mother and left Rebecca very nearly speechless.

But she hadn't really minded that. It was enough to simply sit there at dinner picking at her food and staring at him, wishing she were the kind of woman who could turn Tucker Malloy's head.

It had taken her a while to realize that she had done just that, actually much more than—

Rebecca gave a start as the crisp sound of dress shoes clicking against the sidewalk broke through her misery.

Tucker, with his hands shoved deep into his jacket pockets, the moonlight shining in his hair and a stern look on his face, was coming back up the walk.

She rose hastily, brushed the back of her hand across her cheeks to make sure they were dry, and clutched the robe closer together at her throat.

He stopped beside the house, leaned one arm against it and stared up into the sky.

What now? she wondered, but couldn't look at him. It was hard just to be with him, alone here in the darkness.

She didn't want to be alone with him. She didn't want to be this close to him. Most of all, she didn't want to feel anything for him.

She'd meant to erect an impenetrable shield around her heart, but her defenses had been nothing against him. Within a matter of minutes, he'd brought back to the surface all those old feelings she'd fought so hard to bury. And now he was back, again. What kind of damage would he do this time?

"Does Sammy..." Tucker had to work hard to clear his throat.

Rebecca looked up at him then, and it was his turn to look away. He put his back to her, so she couldn't see anything of his expression, even if she'd tried. His hand raked through his hair, then settled into a fist that was again jammed into his pocket.

She heard the night sounds, the trembling hum of the crickets, a dog barking on the next block over.

And the world closed in around them, him and her, alone in the near darkness of the porch.

"Does he hate me?"

The soft, sad question seemed to drill right into Rebecca, into the deepest, most vulnerable part of her. She clapped a trembling hand over her mouth to hold back a long, sad sob.

It was so hard, so much harder than she thought it would be. And she wondered how it was possible to be so mad at Tucker and to feel so bad for him at the same time. He'd missed so much with Sammy, missed days that he could never regain and memories that couldn't be replaced.

And that's how she came to find herself wavering, found part of her anger at him slipping away, found herself wondering what he'd suffered as well.

"He doesn't..." Rebecca had to fight to keep her voice steady. "He can't understand why you haven't been here."

She hesitated as she saw him tense before her eyes. Tucker's hands were buried deep in his pockets, his shoulder muscles clenched hard under the expensive suit, his head bent low.

But she couldn't leave it at that, couldn't let him go with only those words. "But he doesn't hate you, Tucker."

He turned slowly, lifted his head, so that she could watch as a little light came into his sad brown eyes.

"Sammy's..." She couldn't help it then. She had this undeniable urge to somehow ease a little of his pain. "He can't wait to see you."

And then that long-remembered smile spread across his face. He was simply stunning when he smiled.

Rebecca stood there, absolutely paralyzed, as she watched him coming closer and closer to her. He seemed to be moving in slow motion, coming to touch her. She was sure of it, and she could do nothing to stop him.

She felt the warmth radiating from him, felt his presence like a force from which she couldn't escape. His hand tilted her chin up toward his face.

Then his hand lingered there in a soft caress, a whisper of a touch, one that stole her breath.

"You're a generous woman, Rebecca."

He gave her another one of his blinding smiles, and for the second time that night, turned and walked away from her.

Rebecca's knees simply gave way. She sat down hard on the steps and leaned against the wall for support.

She was supposed to hate him, she reminded herself. It should be the easiest thing in the world to hate him.

But it wasn't.

Chapter 4

Later, closer to morning than night, Tucker sat on the hood of his car, miles from Tallahassee, miles from any place he'd ever been before, and he wished he had a cigarette.

He'd given those up, too.

He'd given up much too much in his life.

Tonight, nerves had left him unable to be still, had pushed him out of his hotel room, into his car and propelled him through the dark night to this place where the Gulf was in front of him, Tallahassee was far behind him, and no one was even close on either side.

For a man who'd finished running from his troubles, he'd done a good job of it that night. Running from the possibilities of what he might find when he looked into his son's eyes in the morning.

As he sat on the hood, he stretched his feet out in front of him and leaned back against the windshield with his hands cupped behind his head. There was no sound but the wind and the water, no light but the few stars that glittered through the hazy sky overhead.

Tucker looked out into the waters of the Gulf, saw nothing but Sammy's face and sensed yet another wave of regret and recrimination heading his way.

He pulled one hand from behind his head and stared at his own fingers, the ones he'd allowed for just a moment to settle on Rebecca's chin and then used to tilt her face up so he could look into her sorrowful green eyes, glittering with unshed tears.

His wife.

Tucker shook his head and laughed joylessly at the slip. His ex-wife. His child. His past, the one he'd left behind but never escaped. It was closer than he would have ever believed, even after all the running he'd done.

And now that he'd stopped running, what was he going to do? He'd been surprised twice tonight, surprised by his reaction to both Sammy and Rebecca.

For a minute there in his son's bedroom, Tucker thought he might die from the pain of the weight crushing his chest. He saw Sammy, sprawled out on the bed, arms and legs everywhere, hair going in every direction, and those heavy, thick lashes covering the eyes Tucker was afraid to face.

And then the room started to spin and went dark. It was too hot in there; he started sweating. And a moment later, it had been too cold.

He wondered if Sammy would ever look at him and smile, the way the boy smiled up into his mother's eyes in the photographs Tucker had. He wondered if Sammy would ever run to him for comfort when he was hurt, for security when he was scared, or just for the sheer joy of being held and loved.

Tucker's mouth went dry, and the weight settled down onto his chest again. Nervous energy pushed him to sit up and slide off the car. Then he shoved his hands into his pockets and started to pace around it.

What was he going to do? How was he going to make it right? He knew as much about being a good father as he did about being a good husband—damned little about both.

And he couldn't screw it up this time. He wouldn't.

Tucker closed his eyes and remembered the way it had been, soon after Sammy was born, in those last crazy days he and Rebecca had spent together. Sammy was so tiny, so fragile, a strange and bewildering creature. All too often the baby turned red in the face and screamed, his hands and fists waving and kicking on those few occasions when Tucker held him.

Tucker was simply overwhelmed by the baby. He didn't know how to hold Sammy without worrying about dropping him. He had no clue about what to do when the child cried, and a bottle didn't satisfy him.

But there was that one time Tucker remembered so clearly, when Sammy had surprised them both. He'd been fussing forever, and Rebecca had been exhausted. She hadn't asked for his help—she seldom had because she'd known from the beginning that Tucker hadn't wanted to be a father. But Tucker had come home late from the office and found her at the end of her rope with a baby who was clearly winding up and not down, and he'd taken the baby from her.

Sammy screamed, as usual, in the unfamiliar arms of his father, but he must have been exhausted because he hadn't screamed for long. Sammy got sleepy, and before Tucker knew what hit him, he found himself holding this warm, ever-so-slight weight that seemed to mold itself to Tucker's body.

Sammy was soft and slight, cuddly and clinging, whimpering softly in the aftermath of a storm of crying. Then he started sucking loudly on the side of his hand and simply rested there against his father's chest as exhaustion overcame him.

A part of Tucker, the part he couldn't let himself listen to, wondered how he'd ever let Sammy go, while another part knew that he couldn't put the baby down fast enough.

And after that Tucker was even more careful to keep his distance because he knew, even then, what he was going to do. He was going to divorce himself from his wife and his child.

So he deliberately held himself back from getting to know his son because, as he saw it, the less they knew of each other, the easier it would be to leave.

A boy couldn't miss someone he'd never known, could he?

Tucker's laugh was a joyless sound.

He was a father, and he certainly missed the son he barely knew. And now that he'd seen the boy, the longing was even stronger. He wished he'd known Sammy as a baby, as a toddler, as a terrible two-year-old, through all the years in which he'd grown to the ripe old age of six.

Six. To Tucker it seemed like a lifetime, now that all the time was gone and the regrets were eating away at him.

It was a night for regrets. Come morning, he would put them behind him. He had to. If he carried them along with him for the rest of his life, they'd kill him for sure.

Besides, if there was one thing he'd learned in the lonely years in between the time he'd left and the present, it was the fact that a man could change. He knew that the mistakes in his past couldn't be dismissed, but he also knew that yesterday wasn't nearly as important as today.

And the past was nothing compared to what he could make of his future.

He had time to get to know Sammy. He would get the time, and he would make things right. He had to, because he wouldn't be able to live with himself if he didn't.

And Rebecca? What was he going to do about Rebecca?

Through the still-dim light of the coming dawn, he stared down at his right hand, then closed his eyes and remembered the warmth of her face against his finger-tips. He could still feel her warmth there, feel the softness of her skin, feel that flicker of awareness that had caught him totally off guard.

He opened his eyes, looked up into the sky, as if the answers might be lurking there among the distant stars. The hazy night was coming to a close. Now the sky was warming to a pale pink, the light streaking across the horizon line.

Almost dawn. A new day. A second chance for him and Sammy.

Yes, he would get that chance.

But what about Rebecca?

He shoved his hands back into his pockets and shook his head. He could still feel her soft cheek against his fingertips. And he knew that he shouldn't have touched her. He had no right. She didn't belong to him anymore, and she never would again.

* * *

Sammy woke early with a tummy ache.

This one was worse than the one from the night before. Even worse than the tummy ache he'd gotten the night Jimmy Horton slept over and they snuck downstairs in the middle of the night to eat the triple-decker chocolate cake his mother had made to take to some fancy party.

His mom had a cow about it. Jimmy just laughed, but Sammy felt bad and not just in his tummy. He didn't like to upset his mom.

She was upset now. Her tummy hurt yesterday, too. That's what happened when grown-ups got upset—their tummies hurt.

His dad was coming, and Sammy was worried.

Sammy pushed the covers back, didn't take time to make his bed or change his clothes. He could get away with that today.

In his pj's, he ran down the hall to his mom's room. Maybe she was still asleep. He hoped so. Then he could snuggle under the warm covers with her. She'd hold him close and tickle him, then kiss him while she laughed.

It was a game for babies, but Sammy didn't care, even if Jimmy Horton found out and teased him about it. Sometimes Sammy needed to be that close to his mom.

He'd never had a dad before, not that he could remember. Lots of kids didn't have one. It wasn't so bad.

"Mom?" He busted into her bedroom, but found the bed empty. Her bathroom was empty, too.

No snuggling under the covers. His tummy ache got a little worse.

Sammy ran down the stairs, calling out as he went. "Mom?"

She wasn't in the kitchen, either. He turned around, then saw her asleep on the couch.

"Mom?"

Worried, he shook her a little.

It took her a while to wake up. She started to smile at him, but yawned instead. She stretched her arms way up in the air, then held them out to him.

She gave him a big squeeze. He felt a little better.

"Whatcha doin' down here?"

"Sleeping." She kissed the top of his head, then tried to smooth down his hair. It always looked funny in the morning, with the ends sticking out every which way.

"How come?"

"Because I fell asleep down here and never made it to bed."

"Like me, sometimes?"

"Yes, just like you." She smiled real big, then kissed him on the nose. "We'd better get moving. I overslept, and it's getting late."

Sammy slid off the couch so she could get up, too. "Almost time?"

"Almost."

He looked at the door, then at the clock on the wall. He'd learned to tell time in kindergarten last spring. It was almost eight.

"Mom?" Sammy thought about all the questions he had and decided what he wanted to know most of all. "Do you think he's really coming?"

She quit straightening the cushions and knelt down in front of him. "Of course he's coming."

Sammy thought twice about asking. He didn't want to make his mom sad, but he wanted to talk about it. Mom said talking about things made them better, usually. But it didn't get better when they talked about his dad. Today, Sammy had to ask, anyway.

"But..." It was hard for him to even say it. "He never came before."

She fiddled with his hair some more, but it just wouldn't stay down the way it was supposed to. "He was here, but it was a long time ago."

"When I was a little baby?"

"Yes."

"And then he didn't come back anymore?"

"Yes."

Sammy wanted to know why. He was afraid he'd done something to make his dad mad. It must have been something really bad, but he couldn't remember.

Jimmy Horton said Sammy's dad must not love him, because he left and never came back. Jimmy's dad left, too, once, for a long time. But he came back.

If your dad really loved you, he'd come back, Jimmy said.

Jimmy was already seven, and he knew just about everything.

Sammy looked at his mom. He'd upset her again. Talking about his dad did that. Maybe he should talk to Jimmy about him, instead.

Yes, that's what he'd do. Jimmy never got upset when they talked about anything.

"I guess ... I need to get ready."

His mom smiled a little, and Sammy knew he'd made the right decision. He headed up the stairs.

Rebecca waited until he was out of sight before sinking back down into the couch.

She'd been waiting for the next questions, waiting and dreading them.

Why didn't he come back, Mom?
Why doesn't he love me?

They'd danced all around these questions at least three times before, and even with all this time to prepare for them, Rebecca still hadn't figured out what she was going to say.

Rebecca picked herself up and wandered into the kitchen. She was going to cook. It would give her brain something to do besides worry about what the morning would bring, and give her stomach something to do besides turn on itself.

She opened the refrigerator to see what she had to work with, then checked the pantry.

She'd worried for so long—started to before Sammy was born, when she knew her marriage was in trouble—about what it might do to her child to be raised without a father.

But the reality hadn't been nearly as bad as she'd feared. She and Tucker and Sammy had never lived together, except for those awful few months right after Sammy was born. He didn't have any happy memories of what it was like to live with both his parents, so he didn't feel the sense of loss that an older child would have felt when his father moved out.

Of course, when Sammy had gotten older, he'd realized that other kids had fathers and he didn't, but it hadn't been a big deal. While it wasn't the way Rebecca would have preferred to have her son grow up, it was all right.

It wasn't as if Sammy were the only little boy who never saw his father. Their neighborhood bore out what the statistics said about fewer and fewer children living in traditional households. There were more single mothers and step-families than there were families where a child lived with both his biological parents.

Sammy did just fine without his father for five and a half years. Then, six months ago, Sammy's friend's parents had gotten back together. Jimmy Horton was right up there with God as far as Sammy was concerned, and if Jimmy Horton's dad came back, Sammy's could, too.

Rebecca dug back into the cabinet for a skillet she rarely used. This was a good day for crepes. Sammy liked them, and he needed something to take his mind off everything, as well.

They'd had a rough six months. She'd listened to Sammy's nonstop questions about his father. She'd relived with him every moment he'd ever spent with his father. She'd pulled out the few pictures she had of them together and explained exactly what had happened when each one had been taken.

And then Sammy started planning for his sixth birthday party. He wouldn't tell her what he wanted for a present.

"Ahhhhh, Mom," he'd said. "Everybody knows that you make your wish when you blow out your candles and you can't tell anybody about it. 'Cause if you do, it won't come true."

Her suspicions had grown stronger as the day grew closer about exactly what his wish would be, but it was only after the smoke cleared that she knew.

Sammy blew out his candles with the saddest look she'd ever seen on his face. He'd watched the clock that night, refused to go to sleep, refused to tell her what was wrong, until the last seconds of his birthday had passed.

"He didn't come."

Sammy had sobbed and sobbed.

Rebecca had held him tight and hurt like she'd never hurt before. And she never wanted to hurt like that again, never wanted her child to hurt like that.

But here she was letting his father back into his life.

It was even harder than Tucker expected it would be to walk up to that door and ring the bell.

Well before noon, not even what he could call hot, not yet, and he was sweating.

He was also fifteen minutes late.

Tucker had driven for miles throughout the night, first aimlessly wandering through Tallahassee, then heading south toward the Gulf Coast.

He drove until nearly dawn, wondering about all the things he'd missed, the precious times he'd thrown away, hoping it wasn't too late for him and his son. He got back to his hotel shortly after sunrise, sure that he wouldn't sleep. Damned if he hadn't done just that, just enough to make him have to rush to get here on time.

And then he had to circle the block three times before he felt as if his legs were strong enough to hold him once he got out of the damned car and walked up to the door.

Those eyes. That was the thought that turned his legs to mush. What would he find in his son's sad brown eyes?

He started to straighten the tie he normally wore around his neck, but he didn't find one there today, then he raised his shoulder up against the wall and punched the doorbell once.

The sound of the two-toned chime was still echoing in the foyer when the door swung open with a fury. Rebecca gave him a glance lethal enough to cut him in two, then stepped aside to let him come in.

She wasn't in a generous mood this morning. She lit into him right away in a voice that was low and threatening.

"Don't you ever show up late again when he's expecting you."

He didn't know what to make of that. Stunned, he remained silent.

Rebecca turned and walked into the kitchen, calling to the little boy as she went.

Tucker heard a flurry of whispers and footsteps across the carpeted floor, then found himself with nothing but the length of the living room separating him from his son.

It was a good thing he'd come the night before, a damned good thing, he decided. His emotions had gotten the better of him the night before. The sight of the boy had torn something loose inside him, some old wound that must have been festering for years, one he hadn't even known about.

That spot he'd thought was so empty, that black hole, wasn't empty at all. It was chock-full of a kind of hurt and anger and bewilderment that he couldn't begin to understand, even though he had only himself to blame for it.

How could a sane man do this to himself?

How could he fail to understand the magnitude of the gift that had been bestowed upon him? A son. His son. A bond that couldn't be broken, even through years of neglect.

The boy standing before him would always be his son.

Now, if only Sammy would give Tucker a chance to be his father.

Sammy stood there glued to his mother's side. If she'd been wearing a dress, the boy would have been hiding behind her skirts. As it was, Sammy had to make do with a pair of cream-colored slacks instead.

The boy wasn't that tall, yet he still seemed to be an awkward arrangement of mostly arms and legs. He had a slight build, a little slouch in his back, tons of sandy-blond hair and downcast eyes.

Tucker wasn't sure what he should do. Hell, he wasn't sure if he could make it across the fifteen feet that separated them.

They both stood there like actors forced out on a stage with no lines to say and no director to guide them. Sammy huddled there beside his mom; Tucker stood by the door.

Rebecca finally broke the stalemate when she walked into the room and urged Sammy to come along with her. The boy looked up, a long way up, for a quick glance at Tucker, one that didn't tell Tucker anything, then Sammy dropped his eyes to the floor again.

"Sammy—" Rebecca knelt in front of him and forced a brief smile "—this is your dad. Tucker, this is Sammy."

"Hi." Tucker was happy he managed to get the word out without having to clear his throat first.

Sammy, still huddled close to his mom, ventured another glance at Tucker. "Hi," he muttered.

Tucker had just a moment to see those brown eyes, and he could see that they were glistening with tears.

"Is uh…" He hesitated, not sure how six-year-old boys felt about crying and having anyone notice. "Is anything wrong?"

The boy looked as uncertain as Tucker felt. Sammy looked at his mom, back down to the floor, then at Tucker once again.

Sammy muttered something Tucker couldn't hear, and he wasn't sure he wanted to hear it once he saw the way

Rebecca tensed up in an instant. She must have heard because Sammy was practically in her lap.

"What, Sammy?"

"Go ahead," Rebecca encouraged. "Tell him."

Sammy sniffed once, then again. Clearly worried, he stared at his mom, and she nodded. Finally he looked up at Tucker. The boy looked so solemn, so hesitant, Tucker almost wished he hadn't asked.

"I thought...maybe you decided not to come," Sammy said finally.

Tucker took it like a fist to the gut. The breath whizzed out of his lungs, and that weight, heavier than ever, settled down onto his chest. It took a minute for his head to clear and for a thought or two to make it out of his jumbled head.

He simply never expected that.

He wanted to protest, to tell Sammy that if his father said he'd be here, he'd be here, that the boy could trust his word. But then why should Sammy trust him? The boy didn't even know him.

Tucker sank down to his knees in front of the boy. Finally he could look right into those eyes, big brown ones with long, thick eyelashes, now spiked together in the aftermath of his tears. Sammy would have beautiful eyes, if only they didn't look so sad.

He took the boy's hand in his and tried to smile, but just couldn't manage it. He wouldn't hurt this child. No matter what. He never wanted to hurt his son again.

"I'm sorry, buddy." Tucker watched the eyes flutter back down again. "I, uh... I was out in the car driving around the block because...I was worried about coming in.... I didn't know what to say to you, or what you would want me to say, or what I should say."

Rebecca still looked murderous, and Sammy seemed puzzled.

"I didn't sleep much last night, and my brain's a little fuzzy this morning." Silence reigned, and Tucker started to sweat.

Sammy stayed close to his mom and kept quiet.

"I was worried that you might not want to see me," Tucker continued.

The seconds ticked away, and they stared at each other. Tucker racked his brain for something else to say, something that could get through to the boy. He was desperate to do that, but he just didn't know how.

"You know," Rebecca said, finally jumping in, "we had a little trouble getting to sleep ourselves. We were thinking about you. Right, sweetie?"

Well, bless her heart. Tucker could have kissed her, but he doubted she'd appreciate it.

Rebecca fiddled with Sammy's hair, trying to smooth an errant strand into place. Tucker detected a little nod from Sammy, and that was all the encouragement he needed.

"I wasn't sure what you'd like to do today. I thought maybe the zoo?"

Sammy nodded, barely, then stared up at Tucker through those tear-spiked lashes.

Tucker held his breath and waited, surely more nervous in that instant than he'd ever been in his life.

"You thought..." Sammy looked once more to his mother for reassurance. "You thought I might not like you?"

"Yes."

It was obviously a new idea to Sammy, and he pondered it for a minute.

Tucker inched closer, suddenly aching to take the boy into his arms and hold him forever and then some. But he didn't. He couldn't. If nothing else, he had learned a measure of patience over the years. He reminded himself that now was the time to take advantage of that.

"I guess maybe you were a little worried, too?"

Sammy shrugged and looked down at his shoes, scuffing one sneaker against the other. "I guess . . . yeah."

And then he gave Tucker a shy little smile, one that let Tucker know that just maybe things were going to be okay. It made him damned glad he came and had him offering up another solemn promise that he was going to do nothing to hurt this child.

Tucker looked down at the boy through watery eyes and wished he'd never left him all those years ago. And he prayed that once Sammy got to know him a little better, got to trust him and maybe even to think of Tucker as his father, the boy would look at him in exactly the same way as he had an instant ago.

"Sammy?" Rebecca said. "It's a little cloudy outside. Why don't you go get your jacket, just in case."

He nodded, took a quick, shy glance at Tucker again and then ran up the stairs.

Rebecca watched him go, and Tucker watched her, watched the slight trembling in her hands, which she'd wrapped around her stomach.

He would have gone to her then, would have tried to reassure her, maybe even taken one of her hands in his, but she saw him coming.

Rebecca tensed before his eyes and pulled away from him without taking a single step back.

He couldn't forget, he had no right to touch her.

Tucker shoved his hands into his pockets, kept them there and waited. Finally she looked at him, and again he saw the fury.

"Don't you dare." She said it quietly, but the threat was there all the same. "Don't you dare hurt him again."

Tucker didn't hear the rest of it in words, but sensed the message from her all the same.

Don't you dare hurt me again, either.

Chapter 5

This wasn't going well.

Rebecca put down the phone and wished she'd stuck to cooking out her frustrations.

Some women ate when they were upset. Rebecca cooked, preferably something complicated and time-consuming, something she could beat and stir and worry over.

She'd started on a recipe right after she'd peeled herself off the door. She'd held on to her composure earlier with Tucker, got it back soon after she'd threatened him.

Of course, the meeting had taken its toll on her. She'd found herself glued to the door for support as she watched Tucker and Sammy walk down the driveway to the car parked at the curb.

Such a simple scene, father and son headed off to spend the afternoon together, and yet it was one that she'd never before witnessed, one that she'd believed she'd never see.

And it was a difficult one to watch.

Rebecca felt a new sense of loss for her son, for the things she hadn't given him. She wanted Sammy to have everything a child could have, and yet she'd failed to give him the most basic of childhood needs—a father.

Rebecca felt battered and bruised, heavy of heart and weak in the knees, all from watching a hesitant little boy take his first steps toward his father.

And where would those steps lead?

Dear Lord, she closed her eyes and prayed. *Don't let him hurt Sammy. Don't let us hurt Sammy any more than we already have.*

She felt tears threaten, and she dared them to fall. She hadn't cried in years, hardly at all since the first year after she'd left Tucker, and now that he was back, it was all she could do.

Disgusted by her own weakness, she headed for the kitchen.

She'd been thinking about the paper mill project, about the old group getting together to try to stop it. She'd been thinking that it might not be such a bad thing to be in the middle of it again.

So when Brian called, she told him that she'd think about helping out with the group. Then she found herself telling him much more than that, things she'd been thinking about for a long time, like the reasons she didn't think she could marry him, not now, not ever.

And before she could tell him to stop, he'd announced that he was coming over. There was nothing left but the noise in her right ear, the angry sound that the phone made when the receiver was off the hook and there was no one on the other end of the line.

No, this day was not going well.

And she couldn't think of anything but Tucker. She'd thought of little but him since he'd shown up on her doorstep the night before.

She saw his face when he'd asked, painfully, if his son hated him. And she remembered the way he'd touched her face; she could still feel his fingertips on her cheek.

God help her—she headed back to the stove. The soufflé was almost done. She'd have to cook something else.

Rebecca was kneading the bread when the doorbell rang. Only thirty minutes later, she noted, surprised.

She'd thought when they'd talked that Brian was in Naples. He'd moved there four months ago to take a new job. She and Sammy were supposed to follow him, but they hadn't yet. They weren't going to.

Rebecca glanced at the clock again. If he'd gotten here this fast, he must have been in Tallahassee when they talked. His old house hadn't been sold yet, and he spent a lot of weekends here taking care of it and hounding the realtor.

Rebecca took off her apron and gathered her strength. She was going to need it, she thought as she opened the door.

Brian took one look at her and shook his head. "What did he say to you?"

"Who?"

"Who else—Tucker?" Brian headed across the foyer and into the house without an invitation.

Rebecca found herself wishing he'd waited until she'd asked. "He didn't say anything."

"Then what's this all about?" He put his keys down none too gently on the coffee table, and she gave a start at the clattering noise.

"Us," she said quietly. "It's about us."

Rebecca was scared to go any further. She'd always had Brian by her side, always, except for that brief period of time when Tucker had stormed into her life and turned it upside down.

Brian had grown up next door to her. Her mother told Rebecca that she'd been trailing after him since she'd been old enough to walk. She'd had her first crush on him, saved her first kiss for him. When she was twenty, she'd been patiently waiting for him to come back from Belize from a stint in the Peace Corps when Tucker showed up at her parent's house for dinner.

She hadn't thought of Brian for a long time after that, not until things had started to go bad between her and Tucker.

"Brian—" She hesitated, finding it harder than she expected and more frightening than she'd dreamed to send him out of her life.

He'd simply always been there for her, and she couldn't imagine life without him somewhere close by.

"Don't say it, Rebecca." Brian started across the room to her.

She backed away. She couldn't do this if he was holding her. "I have to. I'm sorry, but—"

"Don't."

And before she could object, he had her in his arms, had his mouth covering hers in a slow, soothing kiss. Rebecca closed her eyes and tried to lose herself in his touch, but she just couldn't. Brian must have felt it, too, because he pulled away and stared at her, accusing her with nothing but the look in his eyes.

She wished she hadn't been the one to put that look in his eyes. And she wondered whether her life would have been different if she'd married Brian years ago, if she'd never met Tucker.

Would she and Brian have been happy together? She thought they could have, crazy as it sounded. Because she never would have known there was something missing in her relationship with Brian if she'd hadn't already been with Tucker.

But she had, and she knew that something was wrong between her and Brian.

"It's just not going to work, Brian, not ever."

He cursed as he turned away, and she flinched at the anger behind his words.

"I never had a chance, did I? Once that man laid a hand on you, I never had a chance with you."

She stood there, knowing that what he said was true, feeling guilty that it had taken her so long to admit it to herself and even longer to admit it to him.

"You know, " he said quietly, "I was twenty years old when I decided that you were the only woman in the world for me. The only problem was I also thought you weren't ready for that kind of commitment then, and I wanted you to be sure. So I went away—a couple of lousy years—and I came back to find you married. Married and miserable and carrying another man's child."

Rebecca approached him cautiously, touched him gently with a hand that rested against his back.

His muscles tensed beneath her hand.

"And even that wasn't enough to make me give up on the two of us. I was there for you when you left him, there for you and Sammy all these years. I waited longer than any sane man would wait for a woman and..."

His voice broke, and Rebecca wrapped her arms around him from behind and laid her head against his shoulder.

"Brian, it's not that I don't want you or need you or love you. I do." She felt him take a ragged breath, then another.

"Then what's the problem?"

"It just..." It sounded so ridiculous, even to Rebecca, but it was true. "It just isn't enough."

Brian untangled himself from her arms and laughed, a sound that made Rebecca flinch.

What could she say to him? That she was lonely? It sounded so simple, and yet it felt so bad to be so lonely. As dear to her as Brian was, there was a part of her soul that he had never touched, a part of her soul that yearned to be touched.

And she didn't know if anyone ever would.

She looked up to find him facing her again, the pain evident in his face, and she couldn't look at him.

She was staring at the ceiling, so she felt rather than saw his fingertips brush across her cheek to find the tears she hadn't known had fallen. And his touch only set the tears to falling faster.

"Rebecca, if this is the end for us, it's the end. We can't go back to being friends."

She nodded her head to tell him that she understood, then wrapped her arms around her middle, trying to hold herself together.

"Is that what you want?" he asked.

She nodded again because she was sure she couldn't get the words out.

Brian went to the coffee table to retrieve his keys, walked toward the door, then paused.

"Rebecca?"

"Yes," she whispered.

"Stay away from him. He's poison to you."

"It's not about him," she protested. "This doesn't have anything to do with him."

"Sure it doesn't."

His parting shot, she thought, and she was going to let it go by. But he wasn't done. He was standing right in front of her again, and she braced herself for the bitterness and anger she was sure she'd aroused in him.

She should have known him better. His touch was so gentle as he tilted her chin up so her eyes met his, sorrow melding on sorrow.

"I'll go, Rebecca. I'll stay away, if that's what you want."

She held her breath, trying not to let herself beg him to stay.

He looked right down into her eyes. "But I'll always, *always* love you."

And then he left.

Rebecca eased herself down onto the nearest chair. She just sat there, hurting so badly that she didn't know what to do about it, frozen into inaction.

She'd feared for a long time that her relationship with Brian was coming to an end, that she must bring it to an end because it wasn't fair to him. She'd known what she had to do, but when she'd thought it all out, she hadn't thought far enough.

It was selfish of her, Rebecca knew, but she hadn't considered how she'd feel when he was gone, hadn't thought far enough ahead to prepare herself for what would happen when he was gone.

She was devastated. She felt more alone than she'd ever been in her life. Brian had been a constant in her life, an anchor, a rock.

She felt so vulnerable, like a feather fluttering on the breeze. She didn't know where she was going or how she was going to get there.

She had Sammy, and for a while he had been everything to her. But she was a woman as well as a mother. She'd managed to deny it for a long time, but she had needs and hopes and yearnings that only a man could fulfill.

Except, she didn't know if she'd ever find that man. She wondered sometimes if he even existed.

At times her life seemed like a puzzle that hadn't quite come together. There was always a missing piece, a gaping whole.

She had to find that elusive piece that would complete her life, that would bring the whole picture into focus.

Rebecca sat in the chair, wondering and worrying until she'd burned the bread. And then she decided the safest thing to do would simply be to sit there.

She did, accomplishing nothing but upsetting herself even more than she already was. She sat there until Tucker and Sammy walked in the door.

She swiped at her cheeks to make sure there were no stray tears left there and dug deep down inside herself to find the strength and composure she would need to face the rest of her day.

Somehow she made it to her feet and found herself face-to-face with a happy little boy and one stern-looking man.

Rebecca backed away from the sight of Tucker, so tense and so angry. But she didn't get far enough away from him. He still reached her. He found a tear caught on her right cheek near her hairline.

"You missed one," he said, and, with a gentleness that she found unsettling, wiped it away.

Rebecca's breath caught in her throat, and she sank back down into the chair. Her own hand went to her cheek, covering the spot where he'd touched her and knocked her off balance, yet again.

She felt the color and the warmth flood her cheeks, felt her control slipping away, wondered if she'd ever actually been in control, ever, around this man.

She heard Sammy chattering excitedly without really listening to what he was saying. She was waiting, silently, while she watched Tucker, watched him become stern again, watched his hands, clenching and flexing time after time, and she wondered what could have happened between him and Sammy.

"Mom?"

Rebecca finally turned her attention to her son. Whatever the problem was, Sammy seemed unaware of it. He was beaming. He threw his arms around her and squeezed for all he was worth. Then he started babbling a mile a minute about race cars and winding roads. He talked without pausing for breath, his thoughts barely staying ahead of his words, which tumbled over one another in a jumble that even a mother had trouble following.

"Wait a minute." She broke in, and finally he stopped talking. "I thought you two were going to the petting zoo."

"Well, Mom," Sammy said, considering, "we just decided to go drive the race cars 'nstead."

"Oh?" Rebecca looked from the son to the father. "Race cars?"

"Go-carts." Tucker mouthed the word.

"Oh." That didn't sound so bad, not at first. "He's too little to drive those."

"I was driving. Sammy was in the race car with me."

"No-o-o," Sammy jumped in. "I was driving, and he was helping me."

"Okay. Got it," Rebecca said. "Did you have a good time?"

"Yeahhh! We went real fast, and the car made this big noise, kinda like, *waaaaahhhhm, waaaaaaahhhhm...*"

"Okay," Rebecca said.

"And I gotta go tell Jimmy Horton. *His* dad never took him to ride a race car."

Sammy ran for the phone, and Rebecca reluctantly turned back to Tucker, who looked as stern as ever.

She wasn't sure she wanted to know why Tucker seemed so angry, but was afraid she wouldn't have a choice in the matter.

Sammy invited Tucker to dinner, and Rebecca didn't see a way to take back the invitation that her son had already extended. Besides, it was a good excuse to cook out some more tension.

Tucker and Sammy went out to the backyard to play while she cooked and brooded, ignoring the soufflé she'd put in the freezer this afternoon in favor of something else. Shrimp creole, she decided, over white rice. But the cooking didn't help. She feared nothing would tonight.

She survived dinner, didn't eat a bite, put Sammy to bed and left him with his father to read the bedtime story.

Then Rebecca decided to have a drink, a mistake she recognized the minute the first sip of her gin and tonic hit her stomach. Alcohol and old ulcers didn't mix well.

The heavy crystal glass banged against the table as she sat it down quickly and unsteadily so she could press a hand against her aching midsection. Tears stung her eyes, and the alcohol burned in her stomach. She wondered if her ulcer really was returning or whether she was just a nervous wreck, so much so that it was simply nerves eating at her stomach.

What a mess, she thought as she leaned over the table. She waited for the pain to go away as she wondered what had brought her ex-husband back into their lives and what kind of damage he would do this time.

"Rebecca? Are you all right?"

She braced herself against the table and took a long, steadying breath, then straightened and turned to face him.

He was standing in the hallway, looking as uneasy and unsteady as she felt and angrier than she'd ever seen him.

Her perfectly rotten day was going to get worse.

"Is Sammy asleep?" she said, choosing not to answer his first question.

"Yes."

Rebecca watched him for a minute, wondering if she could get rid of him without facing the confrontation she felt was coming.

Probably not, she thought dismally.

She rudely turned her back on him and headed for the kitchen without saying a word. She could finish loading the dishwasher and wipe down the stove and the countertops. It would give her something to do besides watch him and wait.

She loaded the last dish and turned to get the dishwasher detergent and nearly bumped into Tucker.

He had his wallet out, and he was peeling off twenty dollar bills into a neat stack on the countertop.

"Sammy's ready for a new bike," he said as he added another bill to the stack. "The one he has now is for babies. Jimmy Horton said so."

"Well, Jimmy Horton should know."

"I couldn't say, but in this case Jimmy Horton happens to be right. Sammy's ready for a bigger bike. He wants a red one with big tires, a mountain bike, I think from his description. What do you figure one costs?" Tucker counted the bills again and added two more twenties. "Will you get it for him?"

She didn't know what to say, didn't understand why it was so important to him. "Why don't you take him yourself tomorrow after soccer?"

He pushed the money toward her and finally raised his eyes to hers. "Because you can't buy love, Rebecca."

Her cheeks burned. She hadn't been sure he'd ever understood that she hadn't cared for the money he made and the things he bought her. She'd wanted him, wanted his love and his attention more than any piece of jewelry or clothing he gave her.

"It's just a bike," she said, wanting to stay in the present and not the past.

"You get it for him. You can tell him it's a late birthday present."

"All right." She took the money.

"Tell me about the birthday, Rebecca."

Something about his voice tipped her off, and she stared at him. He wasn't as good at hiding his feelings as he used to be, or maybe, right now, he wasn't even trying.

The man she'd married had been a happy-go-lucky type—smiling, joking, laughing his way through life, adept at avoiding a fight and at giving the impression that nothing touched him deeply.

For the longest time, she'd believed that nothing ever affected him, that he didn't care that much about anything or anyone except himself.

She wondered now if she could have been wrong about that—or if it was possible for someone to change that much.

"Why are you here, Tucker?"

She was afraid to ask, afraid to know, but didn't see how she could avoid it any longer.

"The birthday," he said quietly, dangerously quietly. "Your mother sends me a picture every year from his birthday and another one from Christmas."

Rebecca stiffened in surprise. She hadn't known that, couldn't imagine Tucker looking in on their lives that way, couldn't imagine that he'd even want to do as much as look at a picture every six months.

"Why?" she asked finally, because she couldn't manage more than that.

"Why does Margaret send them? I don't know. It seemed important to her, so I let her send them."

Rebecca had a million questions. What had he seen? What had he felt? How had he stayed away after merely catching a glimpse of Sammy? Wouldn't he even be curious enough to want to meet his son after all this time had passed?

Or was that what had brought him today—mere curiosity? She had to know.

"Tucker, why are you here?" she repeated.

"I think you know."

She shook her head and said, "No." She'd never even begun to understand him.

"Where are your pictures from his birthday?" he asked, his tone frightening her.

"In the album on the bookshelf in the living room."

He was heading that way even as she finished telling him where to find them. She walked briskly behind him and with a sinking feeling believed she knew what he had seen, that she already knew what he knew now.

"This one?" he said with his hand on a thick three-ring binder of photographs.

"No. We filled up that one when he was a baby. This one." She went to grab a thinner binder from the shelf and got too close to him, found herself brushing up against him, the brief contact unsettling her as much as the look in his eyes.

They both backed away from each other and stared. Just a touch, her right side against the hard wall of his chest, nothing that should set her pulse to racing, even if she was as nervous as a cat.

What was this man doing to her? What was he after? And how was she going to protect herself this time?

She moved quickly to the sofa and sat the picture album down, unopened, on the coffee table. Then she stared at the floor and prayed she was wrong about what he was looking for inside.

The sofa cushion to her right sagged as Tucker sat down beside her. He flipped to the back of the album, guessing correctly that the birthday photos were the most recent ones put inside.

"There," he said bluntly as he punched the picture with his index finger. "What do you see?"

A terribly sad little boy.

She didn't even have to look down to the picture he'd picked. She knew the one. Sammy, sad as could be, facing seven glowing birthday candles and looking as if he were about to cry.

She couldn't stand seeing that look on his face. She'd known the instant he'd closed his eyes and blown out the candles what Sammy had wished—for his father to come for his birthday.

It had been one of the worst days of her life, and it had been the first time that Sammy had wanted something, wanted it desperately, and Rebecca hadn't been able to give it to him.

That was the worst feeling a mother ever knew—wanting to give her child something she couldn't.

"Look at that." Tucker punched the picture again with his finger. "What's the matter with him, Rebecca? Can you tell me?"

She shook her head sadly, hating what had happened, hating having to tell him about it. "He got this idea in his head that you were coming to his birthday party."

"And?"

"And he was pretty upset when you didn't come, after all."

Tucker laughed bitterly and got to his feet. He paced, hampered by the small space with too much furniture crammed into it.

"So you just let him wait for me to come when you knew I wasn't?"

"No." She jumped at his harsh tone. "I didn't know, Tucker. He wouldn't tell me what he wanted for his birthday until that night, right before he went to sleep, when you weren't there."

Tucker scowled and paced some more.

"It was that damned Jimmy Horton," she said. "His parents separated, and then they got back together. And it gave Sammy the idea that you might come back, too."

When he looked as dangerous as ever, Rebecca kept talking.

"He didn't . . . It's not like he begged me to find you and ask you to come to see him, Tucker. He didn't even tell me he wanted to see you until that night after the party."

"So why didn't you call me?"

His words hung in the air, and she paused, knowing they'd reached the heart of the matter.

And she wanted to hurt him then. She knew it was wrong, knew it wouldn't solve anything, but she wanted him to have a taste of the pain he'd caused her and Sammy.

"Why, Rebecca? Why couldn't you just call me and tell me?"

"Would it have mattered to you?"

He halted, almost in mid-step, and she heard the breath whiz out of his lungs.

She'd wounded him and found no pleasure in it. "Tucker—"

"It would have mattered."

She heard the anguish in his voice, and she hardened her heart against it.

"You're telling me that if I had called, you would have come running?" She couldn't believe that. "It's been years, Tucker. Years without so much as a word from you. He's your son, for God's sake, and you haven't seen him in years."

Tucker sat down on the edge of the coffee table right in front of her, and took both her hands in his. She would have resisted, should have, but there was something in his eyes that stopped her, something urgent, something unfathomable that touched her in the core of her being.

"Tucker—"

He held fast to her hands when she would have drawn away, held her and ran the pad of his thumbs back and forth over the back of her hands to calm her, and she let him. She sat there with her hands in his, closer to him than she needed to be, feeling that old familiar power that once sprang between them.

She'd been drawn to him once, inevitably, inexplicably, undeniably, and for the life of her she couldn't understand why it had all happened.

Except, of course, for Sammy.

There was a time when Rebecca had wished vehemently that she'd never met Tucker. But that hadn't lasted. Tucker had given her Sammy, and Sammy meant the world to her. So as Rebecca saw it, she was meant to have Sammy; they were meant to be together. So that must mean she was fated to fall in love with Tucker and have get her heart broken by him.

Asking why didn't do any good. It never did. Fate was fate. It didn't take kindly to questions, and it always won out in the end.

But why? She sobbed inside with the question. Why did it have to be Tucker? Why did he have to come back? Why did her whole body go warm all over in remembrance of him when he was doing nothing but holding her hands and making her miserable, all at the same time?

"Rebecca?"

She met his eyes, when she shouldn't have. She let her hands stay there in the warmth of his hold, when she should have known better.

"I just..." Tucker faltered, and she thought that was so unlike him to be the least bit unsure of himself. "I honestly thought he'd be better off without me."

She bit her lip, bit down hard and found herself trembling, her hands still in his and tears running down her face.

She should hate him. She had for years, and one heartfelt confession couldn't change that but—oh, a part of her hurt so badly for him then. Hurt for him, and at the same time, blamed him. She tried to concentrate on the anger and to hang on to the need to blame him. She had to do that.

"It's just not enough, Tucker. It's a cop-out."

"I know," he admitted. "But it's true."

Well, maybe it was. It was probably true. Rebecca couldn't deny that. And she believed Tucker, believed that he honestly did think Sammy had been better off without him. And it just wasn't fair. It was so absolutely unfair that it had happened this way and that there'd been so much hurt and so much pain to go around.

And grudgingly, she had to admit that part of the hurt had come from the knowledge that it wasn't just him to blame. She'd blamed Tucker for years for the mess they'd made of their family, and sometimes when she was being really honest with herself, she blamed herself as well.

Usually, it was easy to bury that self-blame deep inside, but not tonight.

She'd failed, too. She'd chosen poorly when she'd agreed to become Tucker's wife and made an even greater error in thinking that a child might help hold that troubled marriage together.

It had been terribly unfair to Sammy. He deserved the very best she had to give him, and as Rebecca saw it, the best gift a mother could give her son was to bring him into the world in the midst of a strong, loving marriage.

She hadn't given her son that.

Rebecca almost wept then. She could have collapsed on the floor and dissolved into a puddle at Tucker's feet and wept.

The sadness was just too much, too big, too overwhelming. How much of it could one person take?

It was so much easier when the past stayed in the past, when she could think of Tucker as this cold, unfeeling person. It was easier to hate him and then try to push him from her mind and from their lives.

Why did he have to come back and bring up all these things in their shared past? Why?

He caught her unaware, lost in her thoughts and her unanswered questions, and before she could stop him, he'd caught another tear as it ran down her face. He was wiping her tears away, again.

But there'd been so many nights when she'd cried her eyes out and he'd been nowhere to be found. She remembered. She had to, because she was sure he was the most dangerous man she'd ever met.

He touched her where no one else had. He connected with her on some level that no one had ever reached. Why did it have to be that way between them, still, after all these years? she wondered.

"I can't do this, Tucker."

She backed away nervously, as far as she could from her seat on the sofa, and when it wasn't far enough, she got up and backed up against the wall and held up her hands to warn him off.

"I don't want to be here with you. I don't want you to try to explain things to me or to make me understand, and I don't want you to touch me again."

She was revealing much more than she should have to him with her plea, but she didn't care. She just couldn't take any more. "I can't be here with you like this. It's too hard. It hurts too much, and it won't change anything, anyway."

He stared at her from across the room, and she was grateful for the distance, although it did little to diminish the power he had over her.

"I just can't do it, Tucker."

He watched her for the longest time, watched her as if he were trying to look deep inside her and know all her secret thoughts. And just when she'd decided he wasn't going to back away, he did.

"All right," he said.

He went to the door, and she breathed a little easier. He opened it, and she felt some semblance of self-control again.

"I'll see you—"

She backed inside herself a little as he paused in the doorway.

"I'll see Sammy?"

She nodded, still wary, still shaken.

"Tomorrow?"

"Yes."

Tomorrow.

What was going to happen tomorrow?

Chapter 6

Sammy woke early, with another tummy ache.

He thought it would feel better this morning, now that he'd already met his dad. But it didn't. Now he was worried about the game.

His dad was coming to the soccer game, the very first one, and Sammy was glad, but he was scared, too. He wasn't very good at soccer. He was too little, and he wasn't fast enough. He tried as hard as he could, but the ball kept getting by him. And that was just at practice. Today was the real thing, the first game, and he didn't want to mess up in front of his dad.

He rolled out of bed and looked at the messed-up covers. They were going every which way. He wasn't sure he could straighten them out even if he tried. So he didn't. He figured he could get away with it one more time.

Sammy walked down the hall to his mom's room, and she was still in bed. He smiled and tiptoed over to the bed. He didn't want to wake her up. He just wanted to snuggle for a minute.

He lay down right beside her and tried not to breathe. He loved his mom. She was the greatest. And he liked his dad, too.

He just wished he understood why they didn't like each other anymore. And he wondered if it was his fault.

Tucker had been slow to go to sleep in the too-short, too-narrow hotel bed, and he was slow to wake up, too, until he remembered what he wanted to do.

He'd run through the events of the day, time and again the night before and long into the early morning hours.

He was overwhelmed by feelings he had for his son. There was awe and wonder, fear and fascination, pride and sorrow.

Tucker had missed so much already. He wanted so much never to miss another moment with Sammy. He'd been certain of it within the first hour of meeting him. He was never going to turn his back on this child again.

So what if he didn't know anything about being a father. He'd figure it out. He and Sammy would make their own way. They'd make it work.

He would probably screw up every now and then, but he'd make damned sure that his son knew his father cared about him.

Tucker hadn't tried to explain himself to Sammy yet, and Sammy hadn't asked. All the boy had done was tell Tucker about the birthday party.

Even now, just thinking about it nearly killed him. He saw those big, sad eyes staring at birthday candles—the image had been burned into his brain. All he had to do was think about it, and the weight settled down onto his chest, the band tightened, and it was all he could do to breathe.

Tucker vowed he would be six feet under before he missed another birthday party.

And Rebecca?

God, what was he going to do about Rebecca?

Who'd have thought he would feel this way after all these years? It was crazy and it was hopeless, but still, there it was.

He felt . . . as if she were his, still, as if she always had been and she always would be. And that was crazy. She'd ceased to be his wife a long time ago. He'd killed whatever feelings she once had for him long before their marriage ended.

Still, he felt the power between them. He rolled over, breathed in deeply and remembered. He'd been close enough to her last night to smell the fresh scent of her hair. It reminded him of rainwater, always had, always would.

And he had no business being close enough to notice and no business remembering.

But he had gotten that close, and he couldn't help but remember. He remembered the way her body fit exactly, breathtakingly, against his. He remembered her smile, her laughter, her tears. He'd brought out her tears again the night before.

Damn, this was crazy.

He squinted at the bright sunlight shining through the narrow gap in the drapes, then turned to find the clock. Seven-twenty on a Sunday morning—not too early, he thought, and reached for the phone.

The tears had reminded him of sitting in front of her and holding her hands in his, of running his thumb over the back of her hand and her fingers and remembering the gold ring she'd always worn on the little finger of her right hand.

It had been her grandmother's, and she always wore it. He remembered because for a while it had angered him that she wore that simple gold band of her grandmother's yet didn't care for the more expensive, more impressive gemstones he'd given her.

He'd started with diamonds, a big pear-shaped one with light dancing inside it, as an engagement ring. And she'd worn it for a while after they got married.

Then he'd bought the emerald, square-cut and surrounded by diamonds. When he gave it to her, her lips had moved to form a smile, but her eyes had said something different. They'd had a fight—he couldn't remember what it had been about—and he'd gone out and bought the emerald as a way of apologizing. She said it was too big, that it stood so tall above her hand that she kept knocking the stone against things and she was afraid she would break it. So she didn't wear it.

When he gave her the pearl set, she hadn't even smiled. If anything, it seemed to make things worse between them.

So, years ago, he'd spent a lot of time watching her hands, watching that little gold ring of her grandmother's and wondering why she would wear that and not one of the fancier stones he'd given her.

He watched her with her wedding band, too, the only other ring she wore, and wondered how long it would be on her finger.

Last night, when he'd held her hands and breathed in the rain-fresh scent of her hair, she'd worn only her grandmother's ring.

Not his ring. Not Brian Sandelle's. Just her grandmother's.

Rebecca would wear her wedding ring. Tucker was certain of it. That was the kind of woman she was, and if she had no ring, then . . .

It didn't make sense, he thought. It couldn't be. She couldn't be free. She was supposed to be married to Brian. He was supposed to be her happily-ever-after.

Brian had been there the first night Tucker called. He'd heard Rebecca talking with him in the background. And Brian had been in a lot of the pictures, the ones that Margaret sent him of Christmases and birthdays. He'd been in pictures at the house, too, in a couple on the wall beside the staircase and another one on the end table in the living room.

So where was his ring? Why wasn't Rebecca wearing his ring?

Could it be a divorce? Maybe Rebecca had found out that being married to Brian the wonder boy wasn't all she thought it would be.

Tucker's heart beat faster just at the thought that she might be free again.

He punched out a phone number he knew by heart, then cursed when he got the answering machine. He needed to ask Margaret Harwell some questions that he should have asked long ago.

Rebecca was composed by the time Tucker pulled into the driveway that afternoon. She'd faltered yesterday. She'd been weak and let him behind her defenses, let him get too close, but she wouldn't do that again.

She'd been a little crazy, thinking that he'd come back to stay, that she would have to see him regularly as he came to visit Sammy and that she might not be able to stand that.

But she was getting way ahead of herself. Who's to say Tucker would be around for long? She knew what he was like—here today, gone tomorrow. There was no reason to believe he had changed.

He was probably just curious about Sammy and feeling a little guilty. It would pass, and he would go away again. She just hoped he wouldn't hurt her little boy too much in the process.

"He's here!" Sammy must have been watching out the window, because Tucker hadn't even made it up the steps to the door when Sammy flung it open. The boy positively beamed, and all his father had done was return to their house for the second time in years.

Okay, Tucker was here. She could handle that. She could be civilized for a few minutes. Rebecca had decided to skip the soccer game. There'd be plenty of others for her to attend, and she could do without spending a few more hours with Tucker. So all she had to do was get him back out the door with Sammy.

She looked up as Tucker walked in the door and Sammy grinned shyly at him. Tucker grinned back, and they both stood there, happy to see each other and unsure what to do about it.

She waited, unsure of what to do herself. She honestly did want Sammy to have a good relationship with his father, but she was also terribly afraid that Tucker would let the boy down.

"Hey, sport." Tucker ruffled Sammy's hair as Sammy leaned in close to Tucker's right leg, then gave it a hug.

Tucker paused, his eyes closed and his arm gripping the boy's shoulder to hold him close.

It still did something funny to her heart—just seeing them together this way, and Rebecca was reminded of how easily she'd been thrown off balance the day before. All her vows to keep her distance and maintain some emotional stability appeared to be in jeopardy again today. And all the man had done was walk in the door and give their son a hug!

She stared at them together and felt the distance she'd hoped to find being erased in an instant. Her heart was right in the middle of this, as exposed as it had always been around Tucker.

Rebecca was watching them, and Tucker opened his eyes and caught her staring. What was that look on his face, so serious, so intense, so unsettling?

She wondered if he realized, and thought he might know, that he'd been given a very precious gift—a little boy's trust, a chance to win his heart, to share in his life.

Sammy was ready to give him that chance. She knew from the conversation they'd had this morning when she and Sammy had snuggled together in her bed.

It was amazing the forgiveness to be found in a child. This morning Sammy had no questions about why his father had left or why he'd stayed away so long. He was simply happy that he was back and hoping he would stay this time.

"Good morning," Tucker said.

"Morning," she said.

And before she knew what was happening, he was much too close. She didn't even have time to back away. All she could do was put up her hands to ward him off.

Too late. She was too late. His lips, warm and soft, brushed her cheek, lingering for just a moment too long, unsettling her more than she would have believed possible. He caught her left hand in his and held it for a moment longer than necessary while he studied it.

"Where's Brian?"

His voice was gruff, and there was danger glittering in his beautiful eyes.

She tugged on her hand, and he finally released it, but he didn't stop looking at her that way. What did he know? What was he after?

"He's in Naples—today," she added, not wanting to explain that he'd moved there.

She hadn't counted on Sammy jumping in.

"He moved far away, 'n' I miss him," Sammy said. "He was s'pposed to come to my game today."

"Moved?" Tucker turned back to her with a smile on his face. A dangerous smile.

If she didn't know any better, she'd swear that Tucker knew what happened yesterday between her and Brian.

It was wrong of her to want to use Brian as a shield from Tucker, but she was a desperate woman. She would have done it. But now she couldn't.

"Yes," she admitted, knowing that if she didn't tell him, he'd just go find out for himself. "Brian took a new job in Naples a little while ago."

"Yeah, 'n' now he wants us to come live with him," Sammy added innocently.

Tucker didn't look so sure of himself anymore, and Rebecca, who'd been ready to strangle her son a minute ago, now gave him a quick hug.

"You guys need to get going if you want to grab something to eat before the game."

"You're not coming?" Tucker said.

She managed to smile at him, very sweetly, then. "I thought I'd give you two some time alone. Besides, it'll give me a chance to catch up on some work."

"But, Mom ... It's the first game." Sammy looked so distressed.

"I know, sweetie, but there'll be lots of others for me to see."

He slipped his little hand into hers and smiled up at her with big, worried eyes. "But you can't miss the first game."

She was trapped, Rebecca realized. Trapped by a pair of worried brown eyes and mother-guilt, one of the most powerful weapons a child had, one that Sammy wielded like a pro when it suited him.

"No," she said, feeling defeated and defenseless as she gave in, "I guess I can't miss the first one."

Sammy thought he probably shouldn't have eaten the chili dog. His tummy felt all fluttery at first, then it started to hurt. He'd had a good time so far. He'd walked right beside his dad, holding his hand and introducing him to all of his friends at the ball field, even Jimmy Horton.

But now it was time for the game to start, and he didn't feel so good. He had trouble remembering where he was supposed to stand and what he was supposed to do. And he couldn't always keep up with the bigger kids.

There were lots of people here today, too, and he didn't like the way they were all watching. He felt like everyone was waiting to see if he messed up during the real game the way he did at practice.

He looked out across the sidelines until he found his mom. She smiled and blew him a kiss.

Then he found his dad, and his tummy started fluttering again. He didn't want to mess up in front of his dad.

It was a parent's nightmare.

Rebecca and Tucker sat in the stands, each holding their breath, waiting and worrying.

Sammy had finally been sent into the game, and he seemed a little confused. He didn't know where to stand.

"What's the matter with him?"

"He'll be fine," Rebecca said and hoped she was right. "He just gets a little confused in the game sometimes."

"But—"

"What?" Rebecca finally took her eyes off the field and looked at the man sitting next to her.

He was driving her crazy. If she had to introduce him to one more woman at the soccer field and watch them get all flustered and start worrying about their hair or their clothes, she would scream.

Tucker smiled and women went nuts. They were falling all over themselves trying to get an introduction, and then they gave her that look. A look that said, "You'd have to be crazy to divorce him."

"He just looks so—" Tucker shrugged, looked a little sheepish, but continued "—so little out there, so lost."

Rebecca watched him, brushed her hands across her eyes and looked at him again. He still looked the same as he had a moment ago—worried, all because his son looked a little unsure of himself on the soccer field.

She found it positively endearing for all of three seconds. Wait a minute, she reminded herself. This was Tucker. She knew this man. She knew what he was like, and he wasn't the kind of man to get all bent out of shape because his kid had a hard time on the soccer field.

"What's the coach doing?" he said anxiously.

The coach, Bill MacGuire, took Sammy by the hand, showed him his spot and pointed him in the right direction, then motioned to the referee to let the game begin.

Rebecca watched in terror as the whistle blew and every little boy but hers started scrambling down the field toward the ball.

Sammy just froze while the ball and the boys bounced all around him.

Rebecca edged a little closer to Tucker, and she didn't object when he put his arm around her.

Sammy still hadn't moved.

"Rebecca?"

"Give him a minute. It's the first game."

People on the sidelines were starting to notice now. They whispered and pointed at the sad little boy frozen in place on the field.

The ball whizzed past Sammy, and he didn't even try to get it. All the other boys circled around him, scrambling for the ball, and Sammy just stood there.

Finally someone kicked the ball out of bounds, and the game came to a halt.

Rebecca reached out her hand, and Tucker grabbed it and held on tight.

One of the other coaches went out onto the field to talk to Sammy. He knelt down beside the boy to get down to eye level with him, and Rebecca prayed that the man wouldn't put too much importance on Sammy's problems.

The coach left the field and left Sammy standing where he was. The whistle blew again, and for a minute she thought Sammy was going to move down the field toward the ball, but he didn't. He just stood there, looking so lonely that it tugged at her heart.

"Where are you going?" Rebecca caught Tucker as he was leaving.

"I'm going to get him."

"No, you're not."

"Rebecca! We can't just leave him there."

The coach made his way back to Sammy for another talk. Sammy nodded and looked down at his shoes, then

into the stands to find them. Rebecca tried not to look
worried but was sure she failed miserably.

Then the coach walked away, once again leaving
Sammy on the field.

Rebecca found her hand tucked back into Tucker's,
and she gave his a squeeze.

"This happened at the beginning of practice, and I
carried him off the field then. But at the next practice, all
the kids made fun of him and called him a mama's boy."

Tucker cursed. "That's a hell of a way for kids to treat
one another."

"Yeah, it is. But..."

"Of course, it's not anything like having your father
turn his back on you and disappear for years, now is it?"

Shock held Rebecca silent, that and not knowing what
to say. He sounded almost as bitter as she was, and that
surprised her.

She liked it much better when she saw him as cold and
unfeeling, unconcerned and unworthy of the child who
had sprung from the ashes of their marriage.

So what had changed? What was happening now? She
had no idea.

The whistle blew again, and they stared at the field together.

Why? she thought. Why did everything have to be so
hard for her little boy? He took things so seriously, and
he worried so much. Sammy would be agonizing over this
for months.

He'd never hear the end of it from the other kids. And
he'd never forget that his father had witnessed the whole
fiasco.

"He's not going to budge."

"I know," Rebecca admitted, "but look at the game
clock. It's almost over."

They were both grateful when the clock ran out on that play. Seventeen grubby little boys ran off the field to the sidelines and their coaches—all of them except Sammy.

He sat down in the grass on the field, right there in the spot he hadn't left for the entire time he was in the game.

Then Sammy put his head down in his hands and sobbed.

Chapter 7

They drove home in silence and in misery.

Sammy refused to talk about what happened, and he wouldn't even look at Tucker. He did permit his mother one too-brief squeeze.

Next, they tried to bribe him out of his somber mood. He didn't want ice cream or pizza or even a double chocolate soda.

They finally gave up and let him be. When they got back to the house, Sammy went straight to his room and wouldn't come out.

He refused to let his father in the room, but finally let Rebecca come in.

Tucker went downstairs and stared at a bottle of vodka and two different kinds of gin that were lined up on top of the refrigerator.

Not his drinks of choice, as if it mattered, anyway. It wasn't one of the two days a year he let himself have a drink, and it was long past the time he tried to run away from his problems by swimming in liquor.

But he was tempted. He was torn up enough inside to be very tempted.

He leaned over the counter and let his head rest on one of his hands, then tried rubbing out the knot of tension forming in his forehead.

That weight had returned, pressing relentlessly against his chest, crushing his lungs and making every beat of his heart seem like an insurmountable task. It was a good thing it took more than sick fear and guilt to kill a man—otherwise, he'd be dead for sure.

Tucker stood there with his eyes closed and his head pounding, and all he could see was a miserable little boy sobbing on a soccer field.

What in God's name was wrong with his little boy? That was all Tucker could think about. What was wrong? And was he to blame?

Tucker was pacing again by the time Rebecca came back downstairs. She was going to have to replace the carpet if he came to visit regularly.

"Well?" He stopped just long enough to ask, then nervous energy pushed him on toward the bookshelf and then back toward the fireplace.

"Sammy said the coach told him to stand in that spot, so he stood in that spot."

Tucker looked incredulous, and Rebecca wondered how in the world she could explain their son to him.

"Remember," she asked, "when he first went on the field and got confused? The coach came out and took him to his spot and told him to stand there. He said that was Sammy's spot, so Sammy stayed in his spot."

"Come on, Rebecca." He went back to the bookshelf and paused in front of a picture taken at the beach when Sammy was three.

"I know it sounds silly, but he didn't want to mess up, especially not in front of you. And then there were all those kids going in different directions, and the ball and those people in the stands looking at him. He couldn't remember what he was supposed to do next. It was all a little too much for him."

"It was a soccer game, for God's sake."

Rebecca had to count to ten. It was a tactic she used with Sammy, but it would probably work on ex-husbands as well.

"Sammy's... He's very precise. He listens carefully and tries hard to remember everything and to do what he's told. But sometimes it just gets all jumbled up inside him. And rather than take a chance that he might be doing the wrong thing, he just freezes up. Because more than anything, he doesn't want to do the wrong thing."

"What's the matter with him?" Tucker said, very quietly.

She risked a brief glance at him, and the intensity, the fury in him had her wishing she hadn't looked. He'd always been like this. It was never calm or quiet when Tucker was around. He didn't simply get happy. He was thrilled. He seldom got mad, but when he did, simple anger wouldn't do. He got furious.

Most people found some emotional set point in the middle and went toward happy or sad from there. Tucker never found that midpoint. He gravitated to one end or the other.

He was so intense, so strong-willed, so overwhelming. It had excited her at first. But later, it had simply exhausted her.

Judging from what she'd seen over the weekend, he was still the same. And she was sure it made it impossible for him to understand their son.

"Nothing's wrong with Sammy," she told him.

Tucker turned back to face her. "You want to explain what happened out there, then?"

"He's just a little shy, a little insecure, especially about sports."

"He was scared to death out there, over a silly kid's game."

"Well, it was his first game. Lots of people were watching. He just got scared, Tucker, and confused. Little kids get scared."

"Those other kids were fine. It was their first game and lots of people were watching them. They did just fine."

"They're not Sammy."

"No, they were fine. All of them."

"Yes, but they're not Sammy, and it's not fair of you to compare him to the rest of them."

"Oh, come on, Rebecca. He was terrified out there, and you can't tell me it's normal for a soccer game to scare a little boy to death."

She was losing her patience then. She didn't have to explain anything to this man.

"You just don't know him, Tucker. You don't know anything about him."

He closed his eyes then and clenched his fists. His lips stretched into a thin, taut line.

Too late, she realized what she'd said. She'd wounded him, and though he might deserve what she said, she did regret it.

"Look, I'm not trying to hurt you. Honestly, I'm not. I think we've hurt each other enough for three lifetimes at least. But you have no right to turn your back on him for all those years and then come storming in here and telling me there's something terribly wrong with Sammy and demanding that I explain—"

He put his fingers to her lips, singeing them but succeeding in stopping her words. She couldn't get away fast enough, and almost fell as she tried to back away too fast.

He caught her by her upper arms, holding her just enough to keep her from falling, then carefully letting her go once she righted herself.

"Just tell me this," he said very quietly. "Do you think it's because of me?"

"Of you?"

"Because I was never around. I mean . . ."

Rebecca didn't hear any more. She drew deep inside herself and let herself simply feel. How did he do this to her? How did he find that direct line, right into her heart, and tug at her emotions like this. He knew just what to say, what to do, how to touch her, how to get to her. He always had. He still did.

She'd been furious at him for years, and here he was stripping it all away, cleanly, quickly, efficiently. She wouldn't have believed it was possible, but he disarmed her of all the anger she wore like a protective shield and left her open to him, vulnerable in a way she never wanted to be vulnerable again.

"It's not about you, Tucker. I mean, he's been upset the past few months when Jimmy Horton's parents split up and then got back together again, and that kid started filling Sammy's head with all this garbage. But before that he was okay with it."

"Then what about today?"

He simply asked that time. He didn't demand or accuse, and Rebecca tried her best to explain it to him.

"Sammy's just different, but that's all right. He doesn't have to be like all those other kids. He never has been, and he's never going to be like them."

Rebecca sighed heavily. She'd spent years explaining Sammy to other people, and she was so tired of trying to make them understand.

"Look," she said, "I know it's hard for you to understand, but some people aren't born with the confidence and self-assurance that you have. Some of us spend years just trying to find a fraction of the self-confidence you have."

Lord knows it had taken her a long time to find it herself. It had been long after they'd separated, had come only after she'd found the strength to build a life on her own with her son.

"He's just..." She struggled to explain it to him. "He's a lot like me. Is that so bad?"

"No—"

"I mean, I know it wasn't what you wanted in a wife, but—" Rebecca whirled around to put her back to him and clamped a hand over her mouth. It helped to stifle the groan she couldn't hold in.

How could she have said that to him? How could it still hurt after all these years to think she'd simply failed him as a woman, that she hadn't been able to be the kind of wife he wanted.

How could she let him see that it still hurt her?

"Rebecca?"

He put his hand on her shoulder, but she shrugged it off.

"Do me a favor, Tucker. Just forget I ever said that, okay? It... I don't even know where it came from. I don't want to know, and I don't want to talk about anything to do with us. Okay?"

"Okay."

She found the self-control necessary to turn around and face him. She was stronger now, so much stronger than she had been during their brief, miserable marriage. She could handle this.

"So, it's getting late. I'm not sure how long Sammy's going to be up there or... Don't you have to get back?"

"Yeah, I guess I do."

She wanted to let him go without another word, but it just wasn't that simple. She didn't even know how to ask the question, but she needed to know. She would need to tell Sammy something, so she'd have to ask.

"Tucker?" She'd let him get all the way to the door before she found the words. "Is this it? I mean—did you just want to see him once? Are you coming back?"

"Yes. I'm coming back."

He was angry, but she didn't care. This was too important to let go, and she pressed on. "You're sure?"

"I'm sure."

And for some reason, she believed him. It scared her, just thinking about the harm Tucker could do to Sammy if he became a regular part of Sammy's life, and it scared her, too, to think what it would do to Sammy if Tucker never came back again.

"Look, it's not that late, and I have some time before I have to head back. Is there a sporting goods store around here somewhere?"

"Next to the mall."

"Good. I think Sammy and I need to get some soccer equipment and see if we can make him feel a little more confident on the soccer field."

He was nearly out the door when he turned back once again, crossed the room to stand by her side and take her hand in his—the way he had at the game when they'd both been so worried about Sammy.

"Rebecca?"

She wouldn't look up at him, didn't want to see what was in his eyes. It was hard enough to have him barely touching her this way. She stared at the hand holding hers so tenderly.

There was an awareness between them, still, that she couldn't understand. And it caught her off guard, so much so that she just stood there, staring at her hand in his, wondering why she allowed it and how he could make her feel so much by simply holding her hand.

"Rebecca, I wish I'd been there for him all those years. I wish things had been different."

He waited, with more patience than she'd have believed he possessed, waited until she could get the words out.

"Just don't hurt him this time, Tucker."

"I won't." She went to pull her hand away, but he wouldn't release it, not until she looked up into his beautiful brown eyes, the ones that were so familiar because they were so like her little boy's. "I won't hurt you, either, Rebecca. Not again."

He kissed her then. Tucker merely brushed his lips against her cheek, a butterfly kiss, like he'd given her so long ago on the first night they'd met.

She'd felt that kiss for days, felt her cheek tingling on that very spot, so long after his lips were gone.

She felt the sensation still, even as he turned and walked out the door.

Her cheek was warm and tingling from his touch, and she was speechless. She didn't know what to make of his promise. She wondered, was it the guilt talking? Or a real desire to have acted differently all those years ago. Was he just guilty or did he honestly feel a yearning to recapture what he'd lost?

And she wondered what Sammy would have been like if Tucker had been around. Who's to say what her boy needed in his life and what kind of difference Tucker could have made.

She didn't have any answers.

She just wished that of all the things in the world her child could want, he could have picked something other than his father.

And she wished she knew what to say to make Sammy feel better, because it wasn't just a silly soccer game to him. Sammy took the game very seriously. He took everything seriously. And to him, this was one more test that he'd failed.

Later that day, Tucker sat at his son's bedside, stroking Sammy's hair and wondering whether or not he was supposed to acknowledge the sniffling sounds Sammy was making.

He figured six-year-old boys might not appreciate having their father finding them sobbing in their beds. So he just sat there by Sammy's side, stroking his hair and making slow circles on his back while he waited for Sammy to calm down.

And he wondered how many other times his son needed a father and had none to turn to.

Tucker knew the feeling well. His parents had divorced when he was seven, and he'd been caught in the middle of the whole thing. The yelling, the screaming, the tears—he'd heard them all.

And he hadn't just lost his father. He might as well have lost his mother, too. The bitter custody fight they'd 'waged hadn't ended, not with the judge's decision that Tucker should live with his mother, not ever.

They were still battling it out today. Tucker was their favorite weapon. They didn't see each other anymore, but they both saw Tucker. They both talked to Tucker, and they were both still trying to convince him that it was the other parent who was in the wrong in the whole mess.

Tucker had given up trying to convince them that no one would ever win the kind of battle they were fighting.

It seemed as if they'd gotten great joy out of inflicting pain on each other, and either they hadn't noticed or they didn't care that it was tearing Tucker apart.

He'd sometimes wished his parents had divorced him as well as each other.

As he'd grown older, he'd vowed that he would never marry and he would never have children, because divorce had become as common as happily-ever-afters. He couldn't risk putting himself through another divorce, and he wouldn't risk putting his own child through the pain he'd experienced.

Somehow Rebecca had made him forget all his vows. It wasn't so much that he suddenly believed they could make it work as much he wanted so desperately to believe it. She'd blinded him to his past and to his fears.

And when everything he'd feared had come true, when he was sure it would never work, sure that he could never make her happy, he'd made one other vow that he had managed to keep—that their break would be clean and complete. There was no custody fight, no visitation rights to negotiate, no fights over child support.

He'd also believed that Rebecca and Sammy wouldn't be alone for long. Brian had been waiting. Brian still loved her, and he would have loved Sammy, as well.

So what had gone wrong? And what was he going to do about it?

Sammy finally quietened, and Tucker bent over to pick up the soccer ball he'd bought for Sammy.

"Hey, sport? I brought you a little something."

Sammy rubbed at his eyes with the back of his hands, then finally turned over.

He looked so sad that for a minute, Tucker thought he was going to cry as well. Somehow, he managed to smile a little instead.

"Here." He gave Sammy the ball. "I thought you and I might work on your soccer game a little next time I come to visit. Okay?"

Sammy took the ball and refused to look at his father. "Well, 'kay."

"So, when's the next game?"

Sammy sniffled again. "Sunday."

"Well, I guess we'll have to practice on Saturday."

Sammy finally looked at him, just for a minute. "You're gonna come back?"

"If you want me to."

"Even though I messed up at the game."

"Oh, Sammy." Tucker couldn't stand it anymore. He hauled Sammy up into his lap and held him as close as he could. Sammy snuggled into his arms and rested his cheek against Tucker's chest. Two little arms stretched as far as they could around Tucker's chest.

"I mess up a lot," Sammy said.

Tucker gave him a squeeze. "So do I."

"Really?" Sammy pulled back enough to look at his father. "You do?"

"I do."

Sammy considered that for a moment, then looked very serious again. "I'd like it if you came back."

Tucker smiled from ear to ear. It was the best news he'd had in years. Sammy wanted him to come back.

He was going to have to explain everything to the boy, sooner or later, and he wasn't sure if Sammy would ever understand. Hell, Tucker wasn't sure he understood himself. But he wasn't going to worry about that at the moment. His son wanted him to come back.

"I'd like that, too, Sammy.

They sat on the bed together and grinned at each other for a minute; then he ruffled Sammy's hair, just because he wasn't quite ready to let go of him.

"Know somethin'?"

"What, Sammy?"

"I missed you... when you were gone... when I was little."

Tucker hauled his son back into his arms and held on for dear life. His eyes were filled with tears and his throat was so tight he could hardly breathe.

It was a long time before he could let go, a long time before he trusted himself to speak. "I missed you, too, Sammy."

"Look, I've got to go. Your mom says it's way past your bedtime, and I've got to get to work tomorrow."

He helped Sammy get back under the covers, put the ball down on the bed beside him, then fished in his wallet for a business card and something to write with.

"Let me give you this. It's my phone number, home and work, and if you need anything or if you just want to talk to me, you give me a call. Okay?"

Sammy grinned again. "'Kay."

"I'll see you next weekend."

"'Kay."

Tucker kissed the top of his head and turned out the light.

* * *

Tucker wanted to drive back to the Gulf to stare at the water some more. It had calmed him, at least a little, early Saturday morning, and he needed calming right now.

He had a son who was brokenhearted and terrified over a soccer game. A damned soccer game!

And he had an ex-wife who was so angry at him—and rightly so—yet so beautiful, so touchable, so vulnerable, living in Tallahassee with no wedding ring while Brian Sandelle had moved to Naples.

He spotted a pay phone on the corner and abruptly pulled off to the side of the road and parked illegally at the curb.

He'd dialed Margaret Harwell's number at least three dozen times today and gotten nothing but the damned answering machine. His hand actually shook as he fished a coin out of his pocket, and then he nearly dropped it before he got it into the slot.

He punched out the number, wondering what in the world could have happened to Rebecca and Brian the wonder boy.

She'd loved him forever, loved him before she met Tucker and after she'd decided to divorce him. And if it was possible to love two men at once, Rebecca had loved Brian even while she was married to Tucker.

Tucker didn't doubt her love for him, just as he didn't doubt her love for Brian. He hadn't liked it, but he'd been able to deal with it, at least while Brian had been in Belize and Rebecca had been in Tucker's bed.

The wonder boy had returned at the worst possible time, just when the undeniable cracks in the foundation of their marriage had begun to show.

Brian had arrived just in time to help Rebecca pick up the pieces of her life. She'd been unfaithful to Tucker—though only in her heart. But Tucker was the one she was supposed to give her heart to. She was supposed to believe in him, understand him, be there beside him.

Tucker had hated Brian Sandelle, most of all because Rebecca couldn't forget him. And in the end, when their marriage was ending, she'd turned to Brian.

The phone on the other end finally rang. Four rings. Tucker counted them, then waited for what always came next. The damned answering machine. Again.

Tucker clenched his fist and wondered what kind of damage he'd do to his hand if he stuck it through the side of the thin plastic shield that kept the rain off the phone.

But he didn't actually do it. He resisted somehow and got in the car. To hell with the phone. He was going over there, and he wasn't leaving until he found out what he wanted to know.

Chapter 8

"She never married him?"

Tucker sat down hard on the plush sofa in Margaret Harwell's morning room. He couldn't comprehend what she'd told him. Simply couldn't comprehend it.

It was like a bad dream, except he was living it, and he couldn't make it stop. He just wanted to go back to the point where he didn't know anything, so life could be the same again.

It wasn't that he liked things the way they were before, just that anything was preferable to this. He couldn't handle this.

Damn. He clenched his fist and ground his teeth together. Damn!

He was going to kill Brian Sandelle. Mister man-of-his-word, the honorable, the trustworthy, the sweet, the gentle, the faithful puppy dog, Brian.

God, he was sick of this man.

"Tucker?"

He turned back to look at Rebecca's mother, Margaret, and realized he hadn't heard a word she'd said. He'd been off somewhere, caught up in the fury, just thinking about it.

Tucker couldn't bear to think about it. All those years he'd stayed away, just as he'd promised he would, thinking that his wife and his child were fine, living with this ever-so-virtuous man who'd sworn to love Rebecca and to treat Sammy as if he were Brian's own son.

"She never married him?" Still incredulous, Tucker asked again and tried to pay attention to the answer.

"I tried to tell you, dear, but you didn't want to know. You wouldn't let me talk about them." Margaret came and sat next to him on the sofa, then put a comforting hand on his knee.

"Why?" It was all he could manage.

"Well," Margaret explained, "it wasn't for lack of trying on Brian's part. They've been dating, been engaged forever, but Rebecca found one reason after another to put him off when it came to marriage."

"Why?" Tucker sat there and shook his head, feeling sicker and sicker inside.

"I'm not sure I understand myself, dear. I have my theories, of course, but—"

"She loved him." His anguish-filled voice boomed through the room. "She always loved him."

"Yes." Margaret squeezed his hand and tried to calm him. "I think she has always loved him, but there are different kinds of love. Not all of them lead to marriage."

Tucker sat there dumbfounded. All those years— they'd been as alone as he'd been, all those years.

"Sammy..." Tucker had to fight to clear his throat. He was choking on emotion. "Sammy said Brian moved to Naples."

"Yes, a few months ago."

"Are Rebecca and Sammy going to join him there?"

"They haven't gone yet." Margaret actually smiled then. "You know, Tucker, I never believed you simply stopped caring for them."

He hadn't. He'd tried, damned hard, but he'd never managed to stop caring for them. He'd also believed that they'd be better off without him, that they'd be better off with Brian Sandelle.

And now he found out that they'd simply been alone.

It was a damned good thing Brian was a few hundred miles away right then, because if he hadn't been, Tucker would have strangled him.

"Would you like a drink, dear?"

Yes. He would love a drink. Two, he thought, would be even better.

"I gave it up, Margaret."

"Drinking?"

"Yes."

"But that wasn't all you gave up, was it?"

His only response was a tightening of his jaw. Margaret Harwell had always seen too much.

"Why did you do it, Tucker? Why did you give up on them?"

He said nothing. He couldn't. There was nothing to say.

"You know," Margaret continued when he didn't respond, "I always wondered what you and Brian had to talk about that day."

Tucker could play poker with the best of them, but he wouldn't bet money that he could bluff his way out of anything when he was sitting across a card table from Margaret Harwell.

She smiled, barely, when she saw she was going to get a reaction out of him. "You forgot. I was in the office that summer helping out for a few weeks while Lilah's granddaughter was so sick."

He nodded. He remembered now.

"Funny," she continued, closing in on him. "All those weeks there, and I never saw you with that woman you were supposed to be seeing. You came in at dawn, worked through lunch, left long after dark, and I never did understand when you had time to see her."

"Margaret." He surrendered. "What's the point? I can't go back. I can't change it."

"You knew Rebecca was coming to the office that day. She always came on Wednesdays to go to lunch with her father. They'd been meeting like that since she was twelve. He never came home, so she always had to go there if she wanted to see him. You knew she was coming on Wednesday, and you're not a stupid man, Tucker."

He laughed, bitterly. "Maybe not anymore, but I was then."

"So why did you do it?"

Tucker had to admire her tenacity, though he could have done without it right now. Past was past. Done was done. Regrets were a waste of time, so he made no time for them. "Look, can we just drop this, please? It doesn't matter anymore. It's over. It's too late."

"It's never too late."

"Maybe not for me and Sammy. I hope it's not, but...I lost Rebecca years ago, long before we finally gave up on the marriage."

"No," she objected. "You deliberately pushed her away, and I've never understood why. But I'll never believe that you simply couldn't keep your hands off that other woman.

"Tucker?" She moved in for the kill. "I think now that you're finally being honest with yourself, it's time you were honest with Rebecca, too."

Rebecca knew Tucker well enough to know when he was going to make trouble, and when he returned that night, she knew he was going to make trouble.

She tried to collect herself while he looked in on Sammy, but there simply wasn't enough time. Tucker could have stayed up there a week, and there wouldn't have been enough time.

She groaned when she heard his footsteps coming back downstairs. She waited until the footsteps stopped, waited for him to say something, but he didn't. Rebecca closed her eyes and held her breath while she searched her brain for something, anything else, that could possibly have upset him so much. She couldn't figure it out.

"Is Sammy asleep?" she asked finally, when she couldn't stand the waiting any longer.

"If not now, he will be soon."

She tugged at the corners of her green silk robe. She should have gone upstairs and changed while he was in with Sammy, but she simply hadn't thought about it— not until she turned around and found him staring at her in the cool, thin silk.

"We've got some things to talk about, Rebecca."

He was quiet again, so quiet. She always worried when he got this way, and she wasn't up to another confrontation with him.

Playing for time, even just a few moments, she backed into the kitchen, talking as she went. "Would you like some hot tea? I was just going to make some."

"No, I don't want any tea."

She filled the pot with water, then reached for a mug on the top shelf. "Coffee, instead?"

He came up behind her, closing the cabinet only a moment after she opened it. She felt his presence, felt his heat right behind her, and all of a sudden it was hard to get enough air to breathe.

"I don't want anything to drink," he said. "I just need some answers."

Rebecca would have turned around, but she knew it would be a mistake. He hadn't moved.

He was right there, so close she could feel the air coming out of his lungs as it stirred the strands of hair that had come loose from the chignon she'd hurriedly created once she got out of the tub, just before he arrived.

And then, out of nowhere, came the thought that he loved seeing her hair like this. She could still hear his deep, soft voice, thick with emotion, tell her so, so long ago. He liked this style because it made it so easy for him get to her neck and her shoulders with his mouth.

He liked to tease her by nibbling on them very gently. He'd catch her from behind and hold her there, refusing to let her turn around, until she was putty in his arms.

A shiver ran down her spine as she couldn't help but remember a time when he'd caught her, just like this, in their kitchen with her hair piled up on her head.

She wondered if he remembered that now, wondered if he ever thought about such things.

Tucker put his hands on her arms, and she jumped at his touch. God, what had she been thinking about?

He let go immediately when he realized he'd startled her so, and that reassured her for a moment.

"Turn around, Rebecca. Please."

She stood there for another moment, her head bowed, her hands trembling and her heart pounding, while she searched her brain, trying to figure out what in the world was going on. She just didn't know.

She wished she wasn't so aware of him, so caught up in this mess with him, their lives still intertwined when she'd have sworn they'd severed all ties years ago.

"Rebecca, why didn't you marry him?"

Anguish—there was anguish in the question. She closed her eyes and tried to close her heart to it. Why did it even matter? Why was it so important to him?

"I... We're engaged." She lied more easily than she would have thought, then tried to pacify her conscience by reassuring herself that it really wasn't any of his business, anyway.

"Engaged?"

She nodded weakly, her back still to him.

"For six years?"

"The better part of it."

He turned her around gently, with two hands on her shoulders, then grabbed her left hand. "Where's the ring?"

It was in a drawer somewhere. Brian wouldn't take it back, and she hadn't felt comfortable wearing it in a long time. Nothing had felt right in a long time.

"Why is he in Naples when you and Sammy are here?"

She pulled her hand free.

"It doesn't have anything to do with you, Tucker."

His eyes blazed, and his jaw tightened. It was definitely the wrong thing to say. He laughed sarcastically, shook his head, went to back away and then changed his mind. Suddenly he was closer than ever, leaning over her, trapping her between him and the kitchen cabinets.

"I can't believe you said that."

"It's not—"

"You loved him, Rebecca. You married me, loving him. And when you left me, you went straight to him."

Rebecca was too shocked to protest. She had no idea he felt this way, and she couldn't understand why. She had loved Brian; she'd loved him forever. But it didn't come near to what she'd felt for Tucker from the very beginning.

She would have never believed he was jealous of Brian, that he could be jealous of anyone. Tucker was too sure of himself to have the kind of doubts that led to jealousy.

Rebecca would know. She had been the queen of self-doubt, the one filled with jealousy, and as it turned out in the end, jealous with good cause.

"I didn't leave you," she told him coolly, her pride still stinging with the wound. "You left me, and you didn't even have the courtesy to tell me."

Rebecca's cheeks burned. She didn't want to bring that up, not ever, but he'd backed her into a corner, and she wanted out.

They stared at each other for a moment, each backing down. They'd never had it out over that woman. Rebecca hoped they never did. There was no point to it, nothing he could say to explain it and nothing she could do to change it. There was simply too much pain there to deal with.

"I was just . . ." He raked a hand through his hair and looked absolutely lost. "I was sure you wanted him, that you'd marry him and he'd be a father to Sammy. Why didn't you marry him, Rebecca?"

She nodded, beginning to understand now. He wanted Brian to be the father that he could never be to Sammy. She'd wanted that, too. Truth be told, it was one of the reasons she'd tried for so long to make her relationship with Brian work out—because she wanted very much for Sammy to have a father.

Yet she hadn't been able to bring herself to marry him, and she wasn't about to explain her reasons to Tucker.

After all, what could she say? That Brian wasn't Tucker? That he didn't make her feel the way Tucker made her feel? That she just didn't love him the way she'd loved Tucker?

No, she couldn't begin to explain it to him. There was no way she was going to reveal that much of herself to Tucker.

"I just can't talk about this with you. I won't."

"You loved him, Rebecca. You took my name. You wore my ring. You slept in my bed, but you loved him—"

"I loved you," she admitted, because it was true and because she thought that maybe he needed to hear that...maybe now he'd drop it.

But he didn't.

"God, what's the point? You don't have to pretend anymore. I heard you with him in the garden that day, right after he came home."

Rebecca was stunned. She had no idea that Tucker had been there. It had been near the end, when she'd almost given up on her and Tucker. But she'd been pregnant by then, and she'd been hanging on because of Sammy. They'd both been hanging on, barely, desperately.

And then Brian was back. She'd been so glad to see him and so sad, too, all at the same time. She'd hurt him more than she could have imagined by marrying Tucker while he'd been away.

She and Brian hadn't been engaged or anything like that, but it wasn't for lack of trying on her part. She'd thought she was going to die when he left to go to the Peace Corps. She'd been ready to marry him at eighteen, but he wouldn't hear of it. Brian was sure she was too young to make such a commitment. So she'd watched him go, full of hope that when he came back, they would be married.

But she hadn't waited for him. She'd barely thought of him once she met Tucker.

"Do you remember what you said to him, Rebecca?"

She shook her head no. She wasn't sure exactly what she'd said to Brian that day. She just remembered how much it had hurt, both him and her, and how hopeless her life with Tucker had become.

"I remember," he said bitterly. "I remember every word."

They'd been in each other's arms in the rose garden, in broad daylight. Tucker had come by to go over some papers with Rebecca's father, who'd been home sick that day.

He'd heard about the two of them and this garden, how they'd played there together as children. He'd heard how they'd always been together and how amazed everyone was that Rebecca would ever marry anyone but Brian.

Tucker had hated Brian Sandelle before he even laid eyes on the man, hated Brian even more when Tucker found him standing there with Rebecca in his arms.

But that hadn't hurt nearly as much as what Rebecca had told Brian—or rather what she hadn't told Brian.

It hadn't been so bad, at first. Brian had been furious, and Rebecca had been trying to pull away from him.

"Tell me that you love him," he'd demanded.

"I do," Rebecca told him. But it had been the way she'd said it, so quietly, sadly, with so many regrets.

"Tell me that he's made you happy."

And she hadn't been able to say it. Tucker had waited, his jaw clenched, the muscles in his hand starting to ache because of how tightly he'd been gripping his briefcase.

She couldn't say it.

She wouldn't, because it would have been a betrayal to admit it, and she wouldn't betray her husband. But she wouldn't lie to Brian, either.

So she'd said nothing.

And Brian had known. Tucker had been able to see that. Brian had known she wasn't happy, and he'd been hopeful once he'd known that.

"Now," Brian had said to Rebecca, "tell me you don't love me anymore."

And again, Tucker's wife hadn't said a word. She didn't have to. Her silence spoke volumes.

Rebecca had tears running down her cheeks when Tucker was done. She'd only remembered the pain, but now she heard her own words come back to haunt her. And for the first time, she saw it for what it really was— a terrible betrayal of her husband and their marriage vows.

She'd stood there in the garden, pregnant with her husband's child, but in the arms of another man, a man who still wanted her, who even wanted to marry her and be a father to her child.

It had been one of the saddest days of her life. She'd looked at Brian and questioned every decision she'd made since he left, regretted most of them.

But it was too late, she'd told him. She'd chosen her path, her husband; she'd made a child with him. And most of all, despite all their problems, she loved Tucker. She just didn't think she'd ever be the woman who could make him happy.

Rebecca wiped her tears away and took a long, steadying breath.

"I loved you when I married you, Tucker. I didn't love anyone but you."

That mollified him, and as she saw it, the admission was a small price to pay to calm him down a little.

"And I didn't love anyone but you," he said.

Not at first, anyway. She closed her eyes against the pain. It was always there, waiting for her whenever she thought of him and that woman.

"Can we just drop this, please?"

"As soon as you explain to me why you're still a single woman."

"Tucker—"

"All these years, I thought you were married. I thought Sammy had a father."

"And would anything have been different if you'd known that I wasn't married to Brian? You didn't want to be a father. You told me so the day you found out I was pregnant."

God, what a day that had been! She still didn't know how she survived that day, how she got through the whole pregnancy knowing her husband didn't even want their child.

"I wanted you to be happy, Rebecca. I wanted Sammy to be happy, and I didn't think I could give either one of you what you needed back then."

Maybe he believed that. Maybe, but it didn't change what he'd done. A man couldn't just pass his responsibilities on to another man.

"You can't blame Brian for not doing your job. You're Sammy's father. You're the one who was supposed to be there for him."

"I know."

She was surprised that he admitted it so easily. He just kept surprising her, and she didn't like it. She didn't want to change the way she thought of him and of the past.

She didn't want to think of him at all. And she wanted her life back, hers and Sammy's, the way it used to be, the way it was just three days ago before Tucker waltzed back into town.

"Rebecca?"

"Yes." She answered, but she didn't turn around. She didn't want to look at him, didn't want to see the sadness there in his eyes. It seemed they'd both been so sad for so long. It should have been over by now. She wanted it done.

"Remember the night before our wedding, the rehearsal dinner? My mother was going to have it at her house at first. Then my father heard about it and insisted on renting out that fancy Italian place downtown. And then my mother said she'd just hire the chef and bring the whole party to the house, because her house was so much nicer than the restaurant he'd picked."

"Yes." She did remember. She hadn't given it a lot of thought at the time. She'd simply been too excited, too happy at the thought of marrying Tucker. There wasn't a lot that penetrated through the wild joy and excitement she felt at the thought of becoming his wife.

"It was always like that between them. Used to drive me crazy the way they were always trying to outdo each other."

Rebecca remembered that he did keep his distance from them, and she'd questioned him about it more than once. He simply hadn't responded, not with any answer that actually told her anything. Tucker wasn't the kind of man who opened up very often about his feelings. She was surprised he was telling her so much now.

"I remember," he continued, "when my mother signed me up for swimming lessons one year. When my father found out, he said he'd just send me to summer camp and I could take lessons there.

"Then my mother said she'd send me to my Aunt Karen's, because her brother-in-law was a swimming coach in college and he could start me out just right. But my father said I could come to California for the summer to live with him and he'd put in a pool.

"A damned pool? Just to get me away from my mother for a summer. All I wanted to do was to be able to go swimming every now and then without having to worry about drowning.

"You know," he said, laying his hand against her back, the warmth soaking through the robe to heat her skin, "if you threw me in the deep end of a pool today, I'd probably drown. I never took those lessons anywhere, because I didn't want to have to choose between what my mother was offering me and what my father had planned. I was just so sick of having to choose between the two of them."

He was rubbing her back, making little circles there, skimming his hand across the green silk as he talked.

"And I always knew that whatever they offered me, it wasn't about me. It was about them and this battle they were still fighting long after they divorced."

"Tucker, we weren't like that. We were never like that."

"I know."

"We wouldn't have been like that, not ever."

"Maybe not." He'd gotten to her shoulders by then. He was kneading them, working out the tension and creating a whole new kind of tension at the same time. He was much too close.

"You know, all I ever wanted when I was a boy was for them to stop fighting and to stop pulling me apart while they fought. I didn't want to live in two places and have two sets of clothes and two sets of toys and two sets of friends. I didn't want to be shuffled back and forth and hear my mother gripe about my father and my father yell about my mother.

"My father pretty much gave up on being a father to me when I was thirteen, and I was actually glad. I was so tired of both of them and the bitterness and the hassles that I was glad he finally left me alone."

She wasn't even trying to hold back her tears then. She just let them fall. "But it wouldn't have been like that with us and Sammy. We wouldn't have done that to him."

"I hope not, but there was so much bitterness between us, so much hurt and anger. And I wasn't ready to be a father. The whole thing scared me to death, and then there was Brian, who was still in love with you, ready to take you back as you were, pregnant with my child."

He had his arms around her, holding her while she cried. She felt his warmth, felt the strength in him, the power. He was such a powerful man.

"It's no excuse, Rebecca, but I just thought the two of you would be better off with him."

He had his faced pressed against her hair, and he nuzzled her ear with his nose. She started to tremble in earnest then.

"I'm sorry, baby. I'm so sorry. I'd give anything to be able to go back to that time and to be the kind of man you needed me to be, the kind of husband you deserved and the father Sammy should have had."

He kissed her hair, kissed her temple, then her cheek. Butterfly kisses, landing so softly, lingering only for a moment, then gone but not forgotten.

She'd always been amazed that such a strong, fiercely passionate man could be so tender with her.

"Stop, Tucker. Please stop."

He backed away, and she thought she was free, thought she was safe. She turned around only to find him right there, waiting for her, to find his beautiful brown eyes shimmering with sadness and longing.

"I loved you, Rebecca. I loved you more than any woman I've ever known."

She watched in a daze as his lips came down to hers, and she didn't move, didn't even try. She knew exactly what he was going to do, and she made no effort to stop him. She couldn't have, even if she'd wanted to do so.

Just like the first time he'd touched her, she felt absolutely powerless in his presence. She always had, from the very first time.

His lips closed over hers, and she gasped at the pleasure of his touch. It had been so long since he'd touched her this way. No one but him had ever touched her quite this way.

She was trembling. He touched her very soul with nothing but a kiss.

She felt the warmth, the longing, the desire. There was no other word for it. This was desire—staggering, paralyzing, overwhelming desire—just the kind he'd taught her, the kind no other man had ever brought out in her.

This was what scared her to death about him—that he could make her feel this way, still, with nothing but a kiss.

Dear God, what was she going to do?

He backed away, and she touched her fingers to her lips in an unconscious gesture of wonder. Her hand was trembling, and her lips were tingling, still, even now that he'd pulled away.

It was as if he'd cast a spell over her with his touch, a spell that lingered long after he was gone.

He caught the hand in front of her lips, kissed it lightly.

"I feel it, too," he whispered, his lips not an inch from hers.

She just stared at him and stood there, so unsettled that she wouldn't have been able to put two coherent thoughts together if her life depended on it.

What had he done to her? What kind of power did he have over her?

She just shook her head back and forth. She'd never understand.

"Try not to worry too much, Rebecca. It's going to be all right."

"No." It wasn't going to be all right.

"I'm going to be here for Sammy from now on."

She roused herself finally from that sensual paralysis he'd left her in. "Be sure that's what you want, Tucker. Be very sure. Because I won't have you hurting him all over again."

PLAY
SILHOUETTE'S

LUCKY HEARTS

GAME

AND GET

★ FREE BOOKS

★ A FREE CRYSTAL
  PENDANT NECKLACE

★ AND MUCH MORE

TURN THE PAGE AND
DEAL YOURSELF IN

PLAY "LUCKY HEARTS" AND GET ...

★ Exciting Silhouette Intimate Moments® novels — FREE

★ Plus a Crystal Pendant Necklace — FREE

THEN CONTINUE YOUR LUCKY STREAK WITH A SWEETHEART OF A DEAL

1. Play Lucky Hearts as instructed on the opposite page.

2. Send back this card and you'll receive brand-new Silhouette Intimate Moments novels. These books have a cover price of $3.50 each, but they are yours to keep absolutely free.

3. There's no catch. You're under no obligation to buy anything. We charge nothing — ZERO — for your first shipment. And you don't have to make any minimum number of purchases — not even one!

4. The fact is thousands of readers enjoy receiving books by mail from the Silhouette Reader Service. They like the convenience of home delivery...they like getting the best new novels months before they're available in bookstores...and they love our discount prices!

5. We hope that after receiving your free books you'll want to remain a subscriber. But the choice is yours — to continue or cancel, anytime at all! So why not take us up on our invitation, with no risk of any kind. You'll be glad you did!

THE SILHOUETTE READER SERVICE™: HERE'S HOW IT WORKS

Accepting free books places you under no obligation to buy anything. You may keep the books and gift and return the shipping statement marked "cancel". If you do not cancel, about a month later we'll send you 6 additional novels, and bill you just $2.89 each plus 25¢ delivery and applicable sales tax, if any.* That's the complete price—and compared to cover prices of $3.50 each—quite a bargain! You may cancel at anytime, but if you choose to continue, every month we'll send you 6 more books, which you may either purchase at the discount price ... or return at our expense and cancel your subscription.

*Terms and prices subject to change without notice. Sales tax applicable in N.Y.

"I'm sure," he said, and she saw a flash of that old charm, that self-assurance, the cockiness. "I'm going to be here for you, too, Rebecca."

He left her there, with her mouth hanging open and her lips still tingling with his kiss.

Chapter 9

Rebecca rolled over in bed so she could see the red glow of the digital clock on the nightstand. It was almost ten. She was supposed to be working on the Arts Center fundraising proposal she had to present tomorrow, but she'd thrown it down in disgust forty minutes ago.

Then she'd taken up the permit applications for the paper mill project. She'd been working with the Citizens' Coalition for months now, and they'd managed to make the paper mill project stumble a few times, but not to stop it completely.

Her friends teased her for getting so worked up over the project, and Rebecca was getting used to her honorary title of "tree hugger." She'd never hugged a tree in her life, but she'd like to think there'd still be a few around in fifty years if her grandchildren wanted to play under them.

She'd been born and raised in Florida, and the changes she'd seen frightened her. High rises, shopping centers, office complexes and miles and miles of asphalt. The crowds, the noise, the pollution—it was turning her own state into a place she hardly recognized.

And if development in Tallahassee kept up at this pace, there wouldn't be any space left.

Rebecca wasn't one of those who wanted everything to simply stop in its tracks. She just wanted a little space, a few quiet, peaceful spots in the middle of the development chaos.

Her group had been campaigning for years to get the town and the county to establish a series of parks throughout the area—just a little space that would always be there to remind people of what Florida used to be like.

She'd taken up the project about seven years ago, near the end of her marriage to Tucker, right after he'd started representing the first company that wanted to build the paper mill just south of Tallahassee.

It had given them one more thing to fight about, and that had been the last thing they'd needed at the time. And it had opened Rebecca's eyes to some painful truths about her husband.

Rebecca shook her head, determined to keep her mind on the business at hand. It didn't seem like too much to ask to want a little parkland in the middle of an ever-expanding city, but it had been an uphill battle.

And it wasn't over yet. They'd gotten many of the parks they'd wanted. The only problem was keeping them viable as development closed in on them. The biggest park was centered on a lake just downstream from the planned paper mill, and it would ruin the lake with the noise and the smell and the chemicals.

Rebecca wanted Sammy to be able to fish in that lake. She wanted the birds to be there, the squirrels and rabbits and butterflies—at least in a few protected spots.

And now the city was about to lose it.

Rebecca read through the papers again and again, looking for something her group could use to block the project, but she just didn't see it.

She finally gave up and put the papers aside in favor of her next problem—tomorrow.

Tucker was coming tomorrow, maybe. He'd asked her not to tell Sammy yet, because he wasn't sure if he was going to make it, and he didn't want to disappoint the boy.

Amazing, so far he hadn't disappointed Sammy. But he had turned Rebecca's life upside down.

"Mom?" Sammy called from his room down the hall.

Reluctantly, she rose from the bed and grabbed her robe.

"Coming, Sammy."

She hadn't gotten a decent night's sleep in weeks—nine weeks to be exact, ever since Tucker had returned.

Nine weeks had gone by. Tucker called all the time to talk to Sammy. He'd come to visit three times. He'd gone to soccer games, helped Sammy improve his own soccer game, played video games, impressed all of Sammy's friends and left the other mothers in the neighborhood drooling over him.

And the soccer field would never be the same again. Women were starting to get their hair done just to go to the game, in hopes of catching Tucker in the stands.

He was driving Rebecca crazy, but he hadn't touched her again.

Not really. Except for the way she found his hand at the small of her back, guiding her down the walkway and helping her into the car. The way he sat just a little too close to her on the bleachers. The way he brushed past her in the kitchen when he walked a little too close.

And he just kept coming back. She found herself hoping that he would and praying that he wouldn't.

Because he was driving her crazy.

She couldn't sleep, couldn't stop the pangs of her jittery stomach or the ache in her head that came from lack of sleep. She'd driven him out of her heart long ago; she just couldn't get him out of her life. Years ago, she'd literally made herself sick over the man, and she was close to doing so again.

At the door to Sammy's room, she paused to collect herself. Sammy had been wound up all week because tomorrow was the first day of school. Her baby was going to be in first grade. She could hardly believe it.

She peered around the door without opening it. Sammy lay perfectly still on his back in the shadows. His thick sandy-blond hair was mussed, and his brown eyes were so big as he stared at the calendar on the wall.

The first day of school was circled in red on the calendar they'd made together.

"Sammy?" She finally opened the door.

He looked up and smiled for just a moment, then gave in to the worried look again. "Can I have s'more milk?"

"All right." It wasn't what he really wanted, but she'd get it for him.

She collected the glass from the nightstand and for the second time that night walked down the stairs and into the kitchen.

She could probably use some milk herself. It helped settle her stomach. Rebecca got her own glass, filled both, then downed two more aspirin that she hoped would help her headache before returning to Sammy's room.

"Thanks, Mom."

"You're welcome, sweetie."

"Mom?" he called to her as she headed out the door. They were getting to the heart of the matter. "Do you think those other kids at school will make fun of me?"

Rebecca settled herself on the bed beside him and tried to smile with more confidence than she felt. "Why would they do that?"

"Because this is Jimmy Horton's school, and a couple'a kids from the soccer team go here, too. What if they tell all the other kids that I'm no good at it?"

She chose her words carefully. She wouldn't lie to him, because Jimmy Horton might well tell everyone about Sammy's problems on the soccer field.

Sometimes Rebecca felt capable of strangling that kid.

"Sammy, you'll be in first grade and Jimmy Horton's in second, so you probably won't even see him. And even if you did, he's going to be busy with his friends who are in his class. I don't think he's going to make trouble for you."

"Really?"

"Really." She gave him a kiss and tucked the covers around him.

"Mom?"

She paused again at the door. "Yes, Sammy?"

"Do you hate my dad?"

Blindsided. *Bam!* Like a board to the side of the head.

Did it ever get any easier to help a six-year-old make sense of his mixed-up life? she wondered once she managed to catch her breath.

"Why would you even ask that, Sammy?" She figured diversion was her best bet.

"Jimmy Horton said since you and Dad and me don't live together, you must hate each other, so I—"

"Stop right there. I think it's time for Jimmy Horton to worry about Jimmy Horton, and time for Sammy to worry about Sammy. Okay?"

"Okay."

She'd spoken more harshly than she intended, and Sammy looked chagrined. She smiled and kissed his cheek.

"But, Mom?"

Caught at the door again. Would she ever make it out of this room? "Yes, Sammy?"

"Dad doesn't hate you. He told me so."

Rebecca walked out the door. She wasn't stopping this time.

"You look like hell."

Rebecca whirled around in the direction of an unmistakable, unforgettable male voice coming from the sidewalk across the school yard driveway. Her bad day just got worse.

She probably did look like hell. She hadn't slept at all last night. All his fault, though she'd never admit it to him.

"You made it, after all." She should have known that he would.

"Too late to see the little guy off to school, but I was hoping I might catch him here—" He stopped and turned her face up to his. "Hey? What's this?"

Damn! she thought, with a sinking feeling deep in her heart. He'd caught her crying again. Why did he always catch her like this?

He moved to brush her tears away, but she stepped aside in a panic. The morning's emotional strain threat-

ened to overwhelm her, and she couldn't let him touch
her now, not even in that small way.

She turned her head away and hastily dried her cheeks
herself. "It's nothing."

His look said he knew it was a lie, and she wondered
why he was always around when she was feeling so vulnerable?

Silly question, she decided, her mood sinking even
lower. He made her feel vulnerable, he and everything
else in her life right now.

Every woman had a day now and then when the whole
world seemed to be too much for her to handle, and Rebecca was having one of those days. She'd had a lot of
them lately, and it wasn't like her to sit around and feel
sorry for herself, but she just hadn't been able to escape
it.

"It's definitely something, Rebecca."

He stared at her and waited—an old trick of his. He
wouldn't say another word. He wouldn't do another
thing. He'd wait, right there, until he found out what he
wanted to know.

But she couldn't talk to him about this. He was the last
person she wanted to talk with.

Rebecca felt trapped, felt caught up in something she
couldn't understand, something that wouldn't let go.

He just kept coming back, and everything kept getting worse.

"It's silly." She shrugged and tried to make light of it.

"Then you should be laughing."

Point for him. She drew a little bit deeper inside herself. Why couldn't he leave her alone, today of all days?

"I guess I'm just a little upset at watching my baby go
off to first grade. That's all." A half-truth, but maybe it
would be enough for him.

"Oh?"

He said it so innocently, so sweetly. He could sound like that, but he'd never been innocent and seldom been sweet. Charming, handsome and a little wicked, but not sweet. She needed to remember that.

"It's not anything I want to talk to you about, Tucker."

"I know." He put an arm around her shoulders and steered her toward a wooden bench along the sidewalk. "But I'm the only one here, so you'll have to make do with me today."

Feeling like fate was conspiring against her, she sat down on a bench, one that gave them an unobstructed view of the children and a few parents streaming into school. She'd been watching for a while now. She couldn't seem to tear herself away from the sight, just as she couldn't shake the somber mood that came over her as she thought of all she'd expected her life to bring her.

"Well?" He settled himself beside her on the bench. The bench was nearly too small for both of them. The only way to sit there was to have his side pressed against hers.

She shrank away as far as the confining space would allow and wondered if someday he would touch her without it unsettling her so.

Then she made the mistake of looking over at him, of watching him watch the kids go into school, and she wondered if he could ever understand what she was feeling. She wondered if he ever felt this way as well.

"Sammy's growing up so fast," she said, resigned to the fact that he wasn't going to leave until he found out what was wrong—and wanting desperately for him to leave.

"Yes?"

"And I just wish I could make him stop somehow. I wish I could hang on to this time a little longer, but it's slipping away."

He laughed a little, teasing her then. "Feeling old, Rebecca?"

"No." More like, used up. She was feeling all used up inside, and that was so much worse than feeling old. She imagined her future spread out before her, and she didn't like what she saw.

"You're what? All of twenty-eight? That's practically ancient."

"Twenty-nine in a few months." She smiled sadly. The feeling had nothing to do with age. It was about wanting things she feared she'd never have.

Rebecca waited and watched the school yard. A young mother came along with her three children. The first boy, maybe eight or nine years old, was running ahead of her. The woman had a baby in her arms, and her third child, another little boy, was pushing the baby's stroller, with nothing but a doll in it.

The woman was calling to the older child not to get so far ahead of them, rubbing the baby's back and trying to convince her other son to keep the stroller on the sidewalk—all at the same time, until her husband caught up with them and pulled the two boys into line.

It looked like chaos.

And it looked like everything she hoped her life would be, everything it wasn't, everything it probably would never be.

Rebecca sat there and watched that woman, surrounded by her big, boisterous family, with a baby in her arms and a husband looking on, and she tried hard to blink back her own tears.

She had been blessed, she told herself. She had Sammy, and he was wonderful. They were healthy and happy and safe. It seemed selfish to want more than that, but some days—like today—it got to her. Some days, she couldn't help but want so much more.

She jumped up from the bench.

Tucker caught her by the hand, and all she could do was stand there beside him. "Rebecca?"

Feeling ridiculous and miserable all at the same time, she looked up at the sky and hoped the tears wouldn't overflow.

He tugged at her hand until she turned to look into his worried face. He squeezed her hand and smiled up at her. "You look so sad, Rebecca Jane. Why don't you just tell me what's wrong?"

Rebecca Jane. She almost smiled at that, almost. He used to tease her with that name. He used it to coax her into doing things she didn't want to do. Would she never learn? Would she ever escape from the power he had over her?

She sat down and pulled her hand out of his.

"It's— I can't explain this to you. You'd never understand."

"Try me."

"I'm just sad. That's all. I see Sammy growing up, and I think about what I thought my life would be like, what my family would be like—it's just not like what I'd hoped."

They were silent for a long time, lost in their own thoughts, and then he started to talk. He couldn't have surprised her more with what he said.

"So you feel a little lost."

"Yes," she admitted.

"A little empty, like there's a deep, dark space inside you that you'll never be able to fill."

"Yes."

"You feel sad, and then you realize you've felt that way forever, and the worst part is you don't see anything that's likely to change."

"Yes." That was it, exactly. "But how—"

He squeezed her hand gently, and she finally brought her eyes up to his. "Do you think you're the only one who's felt that way?"

She looked at him, really looked at him for the first time that day, and saw an understanding there that startled her.

Did he understand?

Could he possibly know those feelings as well?

Years ago, she would have sworn he didn't have any feelings, but she wasn't that bitter anymore. Still, she found it hard to believe he'd also hit that point in his life.

"Why do you think I'm here, Rebecca? Why do you think I had to find Sammy?"

"I—" she shook her head back and forth "—I don't know."

"For him. I saw the picture. I saw that awful sadness there, and I was worried about him. But I came for me, too."

He took her hand and pressed her palm against his chest. She felt his heart beating strongly and steadily, felt his warmth and his strength.

"There was nothing inside there, Rebecca. I thought I was so smart, that I knew exactly what I needed to fill up my life. I had the big house, the fancy clothes and that silly red toy I called a car.

"I couldn't have been more wrong. I finally got everything I'd ever wanted, and then woke up one day and realized I didn't have anything. Nothing I had meant anything."

She let her hand stay right there, pressed against his heart, and she looked into his warm, brown eyes, looked into the face of the man she'd loved so long ago.

It was just as she remembered, and yet it wasn't. There was a sadness in him, too, a yearning. Maybe he did understand.

"It's the worst feeling in the world, right?"

"Yes," she said, and when he pulled her head down to his shoulder, she let him.

His hand stroked slowly through her hair, and she didn't move. She couldn't.

He kissed her softly on her forehead, and she just stayed there for the longest time.

"Tell me what you want, Rebecca," he said finally.

As if it were that easy. She shook her head sadly.

"Tell me," he urged.

"I want Sammy to have a brother or a sister, maybe both. When I was little and went to visit my friends' houses, I used to think it would be so wonderful to have brothers and sisters to play with, to have a big, noisy, crowded house full of kids. I wanted Sammy to have that, wanted me to have it, too, but it's just not going to happen."

"Come on. You've got a few good years left. There's plenty of time for you to have more children."

It sounded so simple when he said it—just find someone and have more children—as if there were husbands-to-be standing on every street corner, waiting for her to come along and pick one.

"No." She'd admitted this much to him. She might as well tell him the whole thing. "It didn't work for us. It won't work with Brian and me. It's just not going to happen. I'm never going to get married again, and that means no more children.''

"You and Sammy aren't going to Naples with Brian?''

"No,'' she admitted.

Tucker put his other arm around her and squeezed her once. Then, when she didn't protest, he did it again.

He was glad her head was on his shoulder, because he couldn't help the huge grin that spread across his face, and it wouldn't do to have her see it. He didn't want to frighten her off.

"You can't give up, Rebecca. You never know when you're going to find exactly who you've been looking for, and he'll probably want a house full of kids, too.''

"I don't think so.''

Tucker stayed there and simply enjoyed having her this close. He hadn't said anything to her, because he wanted to be sure this time. Too much was at stake to mess it up, not again. But it had been weeks—agonizing, wondrous weeks—and the feelings only got stronger with each passing moment.

He'd figured out what he'd been looking for all these years, what he'd needed to fill up that black hole where his soul was supposed to be, and it wasn't just Sammy.

It was Rebecca.

He closed his eyes and a smile spread across his face again. He liked saying her name and letting the memories wash over him. Rebecca.

He hadn't been the kind of man she'd deserved or needed all those years ago. But this time, he would be. This time would be different. This time, it was going to work.

"Rebecca?''

"Hmmm?'' She was still right there, resting against his side with her head on his shoulder.

He pulled away, just enough so he could look down into her eyes. "I wish I could have given you that six years ago."

And then he held his tongue. There would be time enough to beg forgiveness for the past and make promises about the future.

Chapter 10

A month later, Rebecca squeezed her Acura sedan into a space in the downtown parking garage and reluctantly headed for the Clairmont Hotel.

She was nervous.

The state's Coastal Commission was one of the last agencies left that would have to issue permits for the paper mill if it was to go forward.

As luck would have it, the governor had just named three new members to the commission. And while Rebecca was away on business this past week, she'd heard that the commission had finally hired a new attorney.

Her mission today was to figure out where those people stood on the project.

Rebecca didn't care for the direction the state's environmental agencies had taken under the present governor, and she was afraid that anyone he appointed would be predisposed to come down on the side of jobs over all else.

She finally reached the main entrance to the hotel and started searching the lobby for directions to the proper meeting room.

She was worried about these new members. Three votes on the pro-development side would be enough to swing the commission in the wrong direction. And the attorney could be just as critical. His tolerance for legal risks and his willingness to fight would go a long way toward determining whether the commission stood up and fought or rolled over to industry.

She finally found the meeting announcements and saw that the reception was being held in the Parker Room. It was supposed to be a party to say goodbye to the old commission members and welcome the new ones, but she intended to work.

Parker Room? Since the hotel had been renovated, she'd been absolutely lost inside it.

"Excuse me?" she said to the man whose back was turned. "Do you know where the Parker Room—"

Rebecca never got the rest of it out. The man had turned around, and she was face-to-face with Tucker Malloy.

Tucker the lawyer. Sleek, custom-made suit that hugged his strong, sleek body, shiny designer shoes and matching briefcase. Tucker the consummate businessman.

She hadn't seen *him* in a long time.

And she'd forgotten this side of him in the last few months, when her attitude toward him had softened so much, when the past had been pushed further and further away, and the present—God, the Tucker of the present was scaring her to death.

"Hi," he said, smiling confidently, a little wickedly. He was up to something, and he'd turned on his charm full-blast.

At one time, she would have basked in it. Now she wanted to run from it. She wanted to run from him and from all the changes he'd brought to her life.

Seemed hard to believe now, but a few months ago she was fairly content with her life. There were no great surprises, no great sorrows, except for those buried in her past, no great worries with which to contend. There was an order and a predictability to her life, a stability that she found comforting.

He'd taken all that away from her. She just hoped he wouldn't take away her hard-earned self-respect, as well.

"Hi." She finally found her voice, and at the same time she started to wonder—just what was he doing here?

"Going to the reception?"

"Yes," she said, and watched as her suspicions came true. "You, too?"

"Yes." He put his hand at her back, guiding her around the corner. "They've really turned this old hotel around, haven't they. The room's this way."

He steered her toward the wide, curving staircase that led to the second floor.

"What are you doing here, Tucker?" she asked when they were about halfway up the staircase.

"Same as you—working."

Working. She had this awful, sinking feeling inside. He probably was doing the same thing she was doing— checking out the new commissioners for the paper mill company, just as she was checking them out for the coalition.

That must be it. She hadn't seen Tucker at any of the other agency meetings or seen his name on any of the papers, but that didn't necessarily mean anything. The company had an army of attorneys, and her ex-husband was one of them—again.

He'd work for anyone who paid his outrageous hourly rate. He didn't care what they did or what they wanted him to do for them. He'd do it with a passion, if they paid him enough money.

It seemed that he hadn't changed at all, at least not in that aspect.

"I can't believe you're doing this," she said, although it shouldn't surprise her. Why would she even think he had changed?

"Doing what?" He smiled when he said it—almost as if he were taunting her.

Why should she think he had changed? Because his conscience finally sent him looking for the son he gave up years ago? Because he seemed genuinely troubled by what had happened in the past and honestly interested in trying to make amends?

Because he understood about that awful emptiness seeping into her soul?

Because he held her in his arms and for a while the loneliness went away?

"I can't believe you're working on this paper mill project again."

It had come out louder than she expected, and as they reached the top of the stairs, a half-dozen people turned to stare at them.

Rebecca cursed under her breath, and Tucker just laughed, which made her even madder.

"You have no shame." She attacked him again. "You'll do anything for money."

Tucker didn't say a word, something that infuriated her, and he knew it, too. He walked straight up to the bar and ordered a drink while she seethed.

Rebecca couldn't believe this. Years ago, they'd had some of their most outrageous fights about this issue. Rebecca had been fighting against the project. Tucker—who had a reputation for taking on the state's environmental agencies and winning—was the chief attorney for the paper mill.

He'd defended the project passionately, relentlessly, tirelessly, as he did all his cases.

He could have argued the other side just as easily, just as passionately; it didn't matter to him. There wasn't a right side or a wrong side—there was only the side he represented. And he would represent anyone who had enough money.

Lawyers, he explained to her cynically, were a lot like high-class hookers. They took the money; they performed a service—whatever the client wanted. That was what his job was all about, he told her once when they'd argued long past midnight and into the morning.

And it had all come so clear to her then. Little else mattered to him as much as the money. Life was like a game to him, and he kept score with the dollars in his investment portfolio.

The self-doubting side of her had reared up instantly, sure that he'd made one of his biggest investments of all in her. After all, her father had lots and lots of money. Even better, he had a prestigious Tallahassee law firm that he'd built himself, but no son and heir.

Samuel Harwell had a daughter, instead, one who had no interest in pursuing a career in law.

Rebecca watched Tucker lean against the makeshift bar and take a sip of his drink.

He was such a gorgeous man, so smooth, so polished, so at ease with himself and his surroundings, yet with a hint of mischief in his smile and a glint of cynicism in his eyes, which simply made him all the more attractive.

She'd never understood what he'd seen in her, couldn't understand it even today. But she suspected it was the money, the power, the prestige that he'd found at her father's law firm.

It all made sense, after all. He'd started working for her father's firm soon after they'd met, been offered a partnership soon after they'd married.

Yes, it all made sense.

Except, it didn't explain what he was doing here now, trying to get close to Sammy. Trying to get close to her.

Rebecca glanced back up at him, saw him watching her with those big, sexy brown eyes.

What did he want from her?

He tilted the drink back and let the last swallow trickle down his throat, then set the glass down on the counter.

She waited, coming closer, while he ordered another and started in on that one.

"Drinking again?" She couldn't help the bitterness that crept into her voice. They'd fought about his drinking, as well.

She thought he drank too much, even though she never saw any marked change in his behavior from it.

He sat the glass down too hard, and the pale liquid sloshed dangerously near the top of the glass.

"Just like before?" He taunted her with it. "Just like I always did? Just like I always was?"

"Yes."

"It's been six years, Rebecca."

So it had. But lately, it felt like yesterday. Those times, those memories seemed so close, so vivid, both the good times and the bad.

She never wanted to relive those days again, and yet here she was, so close to him, her life so tangled up in his. She didn't know how she could bear it or how she could escape from it.

He did that to her, just by being here. He didn't have to lay a hand on her. He just had to be here.

"You know," he began, drawing her back to her treacherous present, "I could hardly believe it when someone told me you raised eight million dollars for some new genetic research center at the hospital.

"It just doesn't sound like something the woman I used to know would be able to do. After all, you used to be nervous as hell at the thought of giving a dinner party for six."

Yes, she had been terrified about serving dinner to his friends and clients. She had always been sure that she'd never measure up. It seemed as if she'd been trying to measure up to someone's idea of what she should be her whole life, always putting up some sort of front for someone and worried that they'd see behind it.

Well, she wasn't anymore. She'd managed, finally, to grow up in the years that had passed.

She could organize a legion of volunteers to raise millions of dollars. She could give a dinner party for six hundred people and not break into a sweat over it.

She was raising a wonderful son, alone, and she made enough money to support both of them. She hadn't spent a penny of her husband's guilt-tainted child-support checks in the past five years, and she wasn't hiding from anyone anymore.

"How did you do it, Rebecca?"

She knew he wasn't just talking about the money. It was much more than that.

"You don't know me anymore, Tucker. It's been a long time, and I'm not the woman I used to be."

He smiled then, really smiled, and she knew she'd given him the answer he sought.

"Exactly," he whispered, as he tilted back her chin with his fingertips and got much too close to her.

He knew exactly what that did to her, and she wished she had the strength to hide it from him.

"Then why?" he asked, so close her breath caught in her throat. "Why would you think I'm the same man?"

She stood there caught in his spell, with his fingertips holding her chin.

He looked down into her eyes, as sincere and as serious as she'd ever seen him, and she simply didn't know what to say.

She didn't know what to do. Why was he here? And why, sometimes, did it still feel the same way it used to with him?

How could it still feel the same way after all these years?

"Tucker?" Jim Gardner, the chairman of the Coastal Commission, slapped Tucker on the back. "Glad you finally made it."

"Me, too, Jim." Tucker shook his hand warmly. "Nice party."

"Yes, it is," Gardner told Tucker, then turned his attention to Rebecca. "And I don't have to tell you to watch out for this little lady, do I?"

"No, sir," Tucker said.

"You don't want to cross her."

"No, I don't."

Gardner smiled at Rebecca and stuck out his hand. She shook it automatically, while in her mind there was a strange sense of foreboding. Something was about to happen, something she didn't think she was going to like.

Of course there was nothing new about that feeling. She'd had it ever since Tucker called four months ago.

"So, *Ms*. Harwell," Gardner said, drawing out the words, "what do you think about my new attorney?"

His attorney?

She stared at Jim Gardner.

His attorney. That couldn't be right.

"I'm going to have to steal him away from you for a while, little lady, he's got some people to meet. All right?"

She nodded. At least, she thought she did.

Gardner turned to go, and Tucker—God, what was Tucker doing now?—brushed past her on his way to follow Gardner, and she gave a start.

"Close your mouth, Rebecca Jane." Tucker whispered it much too close to her ear.

Her face flamed, and the heat in the room was suddenly overwhelming, but she did manage to close her mouth and walk the two steps she had to take to get to the bar and lean against it. She needed all the support she could get.

Jim Gardner's attorney.

That couldn't be right.

She stared down at the counter. There was a drink sitting there, Tucker's drink. She braced herself and took a swallow, expecting to have to choke the whiskey down.

It was cool and wet on her throat, bubbly and sweet, light with no fire.

At first she thought maybe she'd been thrown off balance so much that the taste hadn't even registered. She took another swallow, just to be sure.

It wasn't whiskey—not even close.

It was ginger ale.

Tucker had been drinking a glass of ginger ale.

"Rebecca?"

She slowed down, but she didn't turn around. She didn't need to; she knew the voice. It was Tucker's.

He caught up with her as she got to the top of the staircase at the hotel, and the first thing he did was put his hand at the small of her back.

She felt the touch all the way down to her toes, felt that awareness that had always been there between them.

How could it still be there?

"I thought I'd come by the house tonight and get Sammy, maybe take him out for pizza."

"Fine," she said, twisting away from his touch. She didn't look at him. She wouldn't think of him. She just kept right on walking down the steps.

"You could come, too, if you like."

The hand was back. She sucked in a breath and walked faster. "No, thanks."

"I haven't told Sammy anything about this yet. I was afraid it wouldn't come through, and I didn't want him to be disappointed."

Tucker eased a little closer, just barely. His side brushed against hers from shoulder to thigh, and she tensed even more.

Rebecca didn't want to make a scene. She couldn't handle another one with him. She just wanted to get away, so she kept on walking.

"I tried to phone you yesterday and the day before to tell you about all this, but you were out of town, and the whole thing came together pretty fast."

"It's all right," she said.

"I haven't even found a place to live yet."

Rebecca missed the next step, would have missed the second one if Tucker hadn't caught her. As it was, he barely managed to save her from a nasty fall. He finally got a good grip on her, hauled her up against his powerful body and braced her between himself and the railing, holding her there while her head was spinning.

He hadn't found a place to live. God, where had her mind gone? He hadn't just found a new job. He'd found a reason to move back to Tallahassee.

"Are you okay?" He held her tight against him, and she couldn't move. She was incapable of doing so. "Rebecca?"

She stared up at him, spellbound. He was closing in on her with each passing day. She couldn't understand why, but then, she didn't expect to. She'd never understood him, and she wasn't about to start now.

But she knew as she stared up into those beautiful, so familiar brown eyes that he was after her. He wanted her, still, and she'd never be able to run fast enough to get away from him.

"Just let me go, Tucker." She was begging, but she didn't care. Her sense of self-preservation totally outweighed her pride.

"Rebecca?"

He let go finally, slowly, steadying her again as he withdrew.

She waited there, caught up in his spell, caught up in something she'd never understand. His power wasn't in the arms that held her close. He didn't even have to touch her. All he had to do was be here, just be in the same room, and chaos reigned all around her and inside her, as well.

"Can't you just let me go?" she pleaded.

"No," he said forcefully, almost angrily.

He knew, as clearly as she did, that she wasn't talking about letting her make her way down the steps. She wanted him to let go of the past, to let her forget again and put it behind them for good.

"I can't," he said through a clenched jaw.

Neither could she. She couldn't deal with this—this thing she refused to even name—this thing between them that he wouldn't let go of.

"Rebecca?"

She shook her head back and forth as he came closer still, as the old familiar heat flooded her body and the memories overwhelmed her.

He didn't have to take her in his arms, didn't have to kiss her or pull her against that sleek, powerful body of his. He didn't have to do any of those things now, because he'd done them so often in the past, because the memory of his touch was something she hadn't been able to escape. It lingered in her mind long after she believed she'd left all those feelings behind.

Sometimes it felt as if it had been yesterday—the memories were so strong. And sometimes when she lay in her lonely bed at night, when she'd been so alone for so very long, it seemed as if it had been forever since he'd touched her that way.

She wanted that touch, and yet she didn't. She longed for it, and yet she feared it.

What if all those feelings were still there, still the same, still as strong, still as all-consuming as they had ever been? What if those feelings were still that powerful, that destructive? What if—

He kissed her then, and she didn't have to wonder anymore. Caught off guard, lost in memories that now blurred with the present, she just stood there and let him touch his soft lips to hers.

Gently, yet urgently, lightly, yet demandingly; he kissed her again and again.

She never even thought to protest. There'd be time for that later, once she'd sunk even further beneath the spell he'd cast over her.

The memories and the magic swirled around her. Her lips parted willingly, and his tongue slipped inside just as her knees gave way.

He caught her against him again, between the railing and his powerful body, and she simply couldn't help herself.

She clung to him. She kissed him back as urgently and as passionately as he kissed her. There on the stairs—she was vaguely conscious of the fact that they were on the stairs. And she remembered, another time, another place, their old house, when he'd started kissing her like this on the stairs, intending to take her to bed. Except they never made it, not upstairs, not down.

Somehow—she'd never understood the logistics of it— he'd made love to her right there on the staircase. She remembered the edge of one step, hard against her back, and another against her head; his body, hard and heavy, on top of her. She remembered the urgency, the naked need that had blotted out everything else but their desire for each other.

She remembered it so well, and she'd felt nothing even remotely like that in such a long time.

Rebecca gasped as his lips left hers. She clung to him as the room swirled around her.

"Oh," she groaned, closing her eyes, not wanting to see the satisfaction that had to be stamped on his face.

He knew now. Her reaction to him had left no room for doubts.

She'd told him with her body what she hadn't even admitted to herself—what she'd been too afraid to admit to herself. On some very basic level, she still wanted him.

Rebecca's face burned as she looked down at the wrought-iron banister of the ornate curving staircase. They were in the middle of the town's best hotel.

She groaned again and had to force herself to look up at him.

"Let me go, Tucker," she begged.

And he did. She backed away from him, grateful that he let her go for this moment. But she knew—she could see it in his eyes—that he might let her go for now, but not for long.

Rebecca turned and fled while she still had the chance.

Chapter 11

She should have expected him, Rebecca thought, as she shamelessly hid in the kitchen and listened to his footsteps coming down the stairs. And expecting him should have made it easier to come face-to-face with him, but it didn't.

Nothing was easy between her and Tucker.

She listened while he walked through the living room, through the dining room and then paused to the right of the kitchen.

Rebecca swallowed hard and her whole body tensed. Her stomach was already in knots; it seemed like it had been that way for months now. She felt the knots pulling tighter at the same time she felt his eyes on her, felt his stare.

"You can't hide from it forever, Rebecca."

She wasn't even going to try to answer that. There was nothing she could say. And even worse, as she saw it, there was nothing she could do.

He was here for good, in her town, in her life, day in and day out, for as long as it took to get whatever he wanted. But what did he want? Dear God, what did he want from her?

"Rebecca? Sammy's asleep, and I think we need to talk."

She didn't turn around. She didn't want to face him. She didn't want to see that look in his eyes, that glint of self-assurance. He would get what he wanted. He always did.

But what did he want? Inside, she was screaming. What could he want from her that she hadn't already given him?

There was simply nothing left. Years ago, she'd denied him nothing, given until there'd been nothing left of her to give, until he hadn't wanted anything from her anymore.

"Rebecca?"

"Yes," she said finally, when she realized she'd said nothing at all before.

"Putting it off won't change things."

No, it wouldn't. Not with Tucker. When he wanted something, it blinded him to everything else. And she was afraid, desperately afraid that he wanted her.

He and Sammy had gone out for pizza, and Rebecca had time to reflect on exactly what his move to Tallahassee would mean.

Tucker, everywhere, underfoot, all the time.

He and Sammy had grown closer and closer, and lately, she'd even stopped being afraid about that. They didn't have a typical father-son relationship yet, and she doubted they ever would. But they had something of their very own that seemed to be working for them, and it had definitely been good for Sammy.

Tucker was here to stay. She believed that. She wouldn't be able to avoid him, and she couldn't tell herself that all she had to do was hold out for a few hours or a few days until he left, because he wasn't going to leave.

So they had come to terms.

His terms, she feared. She didn't think she was strong enough to face the terms he would set, but she didn't think she could resist him, either. She was trapped by her own maddening, unexplainable desire for him.

She took a deep breath and started in on the conversation she'd been dreading all day.

"Why did you come back, Tucker?"

"Because I don't want to be an every-other-weekend-and-holidays kind of father."

She nodded. She believed that was part of it. Just a part.

"Because it wasn't enough to see Sammy for a day or two whenever I could get away."

He came closer. She could feel him, feel the warmth radiating from his body just behind her. Rebecca inched as close as she could get to the cabinets and stared at the fine wood grain of the oak.

"I want to be here with him, every day." His hand cupped her elbow, and she sucked in a breath. "I can't make up for all the years we were apart, but I intend to make damned sure that I don't miss anything else."

"All right," she whispered as she braced herself for the rest of it.

"And that's not all, Rebecca Jane."

She closed her eyes as the other hand came up to cup her elbow and he moved to stand right behind her. His hands barely held her there, and yet she couldn't have moved, not an inch. He'd never needed the strength of those powerful arms to hold her. His power was in his mere presence. He had a power over her that would not be denied, one that time hadn't diminished, one that his own betrayal hadn't destroyed.

He came closer still. His breath stirred the tendrils of hair at the back of her neck that had escaped from her chignon, and he set her whole body to trembling.

"We need to talk about you and me," he said, his breath warming the back of her neck.

"No," she insisted, wishing she could believe it herself.

"Yes." His arms slid around her, slowly and gently, powerfully, and he eased her back against him. He enveloped her with his warmth and his scent, with his power. He had such power over her.

"Remember Sammy's first day of school, the emptiness we talked about, the loneliness? I've been so empty inside, Rebecca. I've been searching and searching forever, and there was just nothing that came close to filling that awful emptiness inside me."

She was afraid he was going to kiss her then. She felt his breath warming her neck. But he didn't kiss her. He just nuzzled her with his nose, teasing her, tantalizing her so gently.

He'd always been so gentle with her.

"You know what it feels like. You told me so that day. You've felt it, too."

Oh, yes. She knew that feeling, that ache of a soul starved for love. She couldn't imagine that he'd been searching, too, that he hadn't found someone, that he hadn't found a half-dozen someones to help fill up his life. She couldn't believe he'd been as lonely as she had been.

"I did," she began. "But..."

"What if it was you, Rebecca? What if, all that time, all that I needed was you?" he asked, kissing her finally, at the back of her neck.

She gasped, and her body began its awful betrayal of her. She didn't even move. She couldn't. She just stood there. And when her legs couldn't hold her up anymore, he did.

He kissed her neck, his touch light and teasing, but the effect was all too potent. He nosed the stray curls aside, and then his teeth sank into the cord of muscles that ran down the side of her neck and to her shoulders, and she thought she might die from the pleasure.

"Did you remember," he said huskily, "that it used to drive me wild just to see your hair like this? Did you wear it just for me, Rebecca?"

"No," she said as she stood there in his arms, paralyzed by the desire he'd awakened in her.

"Maybe you will," he said. "Some day soon, maybe you'll wear it like this again, for me."

Her knees gave way then, and she leaned against him. He caught her easily, held her firmly in his arms with his body pressed against the back of hers.

They stood there, pressed together, breathing in time with each other, her heart pounding as quickly as his.

Her head was spinning. Her breasts were full and aching. They remembered his touch so well.

She was liquid fire, his to do with as he would.

His hand moved to the buttons on her blouse, and deftly, he unfastened the top three. Then he pushed her blouse off one shoulder, his lips following the path as it was uncovered.

"I've missed you, Rebecca."

She'd missed him, too. There was no denying it, so she didn't even try. She just closed her eyes and felt the power, felt the pull of the desire that he alone could create.

And then, she knew this was what she'd wanted. This was what she'd missed when she'd been with Brian. This was why she'd never become Brian's wife—because he had never even begun to make her feel what Tucker had made her feel.

She went absolutely still as she admitted to herself, once again, that despite the years and all the tears, he still had this power over her.

Tucker pressed his lower body to hers, and she felt the hard muscles of his thighs, felt his arousal as he settled himself against her hips and then rocked back and forth in a slow, sensual rhythm that she remembered so well, one that simply took her very breath away.

Oh, yes. She remembered.

For years. she'd told herself that it couldn't possibly have been as good as she'd remembered between them, but she knew now. There was nothing wrong with her memory. It was exactly as powerful, as rawly sensual, just as capable of robbing her mind of her power to reason.

The years fell away, and she was back with him where she'd longed to be. He was hers and she was his, at least for these few moments.

She would give herself a few moments.

He rocked his hips against hers. His hand slipped inside her blouse, under the bra, and he found her breast, while his lips found her ear and nibbled on the lobe.

"I won't hurt you this time, Rebecca. I swear it."

Oh, but he would. She was certain of it. He would hurt her terribly. That wasn't in question, but neither was the fact that he was going to make love to her again, tonight, and she was going to let him.

Because she wasn't strong enough to stop him. She didn't have the will to tell him no. Because some part of her had died when they'd divorced, and now it was coming back to life. He brought this part of her soul roaring back to life.

It was bittersweet, the pleasure and the pain, the past blurring with the present, leaving her dizzy with the memories and the feelings.

She shivered uncontrollably, from the heat of his touch and the chill of the memories of the pain. She stayed right where she was, with his hand slipped inside her bra to cup her breast and his mouth in the hollow where her neck met her shoulder.

And finally, when she thought she couldn't stand it anymore, he turned her around and took her back into his arms. Face-to-face, finally, he fitted his body to hers, thighs to shoulders, pressed together with nary a breath between them.

Finally, his mouth settled onto hers for a long, drugging kiss, for another and another, until the room started spinning around them. She held on tight to him, to the power at the center of her storm.

He broke off the kiss, and they both made a desperate grab for air. He groaned and kissed her nose. She could feel him smiling as he kissed her cheek, and she waited for him to take her mouth under his again.

But he didn't.

He kissed her cheek again, then went still. She felt him pull away slightly, felt his fingers reach up and run down her cheek.

Tears. He'd found her tears, ones she hadn't even known were falling, and yet there they were, on his fingertips, then beneath his lips.

Tears on her cheeks, bittersweet memories flooding her mind as she stood there trembling in his arms.

Time stood still and the memories came rushing back, the pain, the humiliation, the loneliness and despair that had come at the end, just before they'd separated.

The memories were closer than she'd thought, and there was no escaping them. She wished that for just a little while, she'd been able to escape them.

Rebecca still wasn't sure how she'd survived it all, how any of her feelings for him could have possibly survived, but something had, something she couldn't deny and yet couldn't face.

"I'm sorry," he said, his voice tinged with an anguish she knew so well.

And then he stepped away from her. He let her go. He stopped when she wouldn't have been strong enough to stop him herself.

She should have been grateful. But her tears only fell faster, and she stood there, cold and miserable in front of him.

"It just won't work, Tucker."

"It might," he insisted.

"It won't. Not ever." She wrapped her arms around her middle and tried to stop shivering. "There's too much between us, too much anger and hatred and bitterness— And I can't go back to all that. I don't want to—"

He touched his finger to her lips and stopped her right there. "Don't you think I know that? Don't you think I've tried to forget you, that I've tried to forget about us, about the way it was between us, the good and the bad?"

She nodded. She remembered.

He wiped another one of her tears away. "But I can't forget, Rebecca. I just can't."

"You have to," she insisted.

"Look, I know how impossible it seems. Believe me, I know. It's all I've thought about—you and Sammy and me. I know you're scared. I'm scared, too, but things are going to be different this time, Rebecca."

He held her easily then. He absorbed the cold, left behind the warmth. "I haven't forgotten anything about you. I haven't forgotten anything we shared. I never will. And I don't think you've forgotten, either, despite all those years of trying.

"Why do you think that is, Rebecca? Why haven't you been able to put me out of your mind?"

"I have," she lied, her sense of self-preservation much stronger than her conscience.

"Then why couldn't you put everything behind you and start over again with Brian?"

She closed her eyes so maybe he wouldn't see the truth in what he'd said, but it didn't fool him. He knew. Somehow he knew exactly what had gone wrong between her and Brian.

"Why didn't you marry him, Rebecca?"

"Let me go." She pushed against his chest, hard, but he held her tight.

"Why? You loved him, Rebecca. He was supposed to be everything I never could be, and you loved him. So why didn't you ever marry him?"

"Let me go, Tucker." She hung her head and stared at the fabric of his shirt. He wasn't hurting her, but he wasn't about to let go. God, why couldn't he just let her go?

"Tell me," he insisted, his voice tinged with anger. "Tell me why you couldn't marry him!"

She looked up at him and knew that he wouldn't let go until he had his answer. He was stubborn enough and strong enough to hold her all night if it came to that.

"Why, Rebecca? Just tell me why."

"Because he wasn't you!" She hurled the angry words at him.

He let her go instantly, and she just stood there, swaying on her feet in front of him.

This was her chance to get away from him, her chance to run like the coward she was when it came to facing up to her unresolved feelings for him, but she didn't take it. There was no reason to run now; there was no place she could run to that he wouldn't find her.

He knew everything she'd been trying to hide, both from herself and from him, and she had no protection from him now.

Rebecca would have sworn that she could never feel more vulnerable than she had when she'd been carrying his child, knowing that their marriage was never going to survive—but she did, now.

She was as helpless as a little baby, trapped by her own traitorous emotions, trapped by the longing she still had for him.

Finally she found the courage to look up into his beautiful brown eyes. She expected to see triumph there. She'd admitted her deepest, darkest secret to him, and she thought he'd be triumphant at dragging it out of her.

But she saw only tenderness, maybe concern, maybe—affection? She didn't dare label it love.

He smiled at her then, ever so slightly. "It's going to be okay, angel face."

And then he held out his arms to her, offering himself to her, to comfort her.

She hesitated, knowing that moving those few inches into the shelter of his arms would tell him more than any admission that could come out of her mouth just now.

He'd trapped her with her own longing, by feeding her own lonely soul, yet here he was giving her a choice.

If he'd taken her into his arms right then and kissed her, just once, she would have been lost all over again. She would have been his, to do with as he pleased.

He'd won, and yet he wasn't pressing his victory.

The old Tucker would have had her undressed and on the floor beneath him by now. They'd argued more than once and ended up just the same way.

He fought ruthlessly back then, with his charm, with his passion, with whatever advantage he had that worked best at the moment, to get whatever he wanted at the moment.

This man standing before her, holding out his arms to her in silent invitation, the one waiting for her to decide what she wanted, even though he knew exactly what he wanted and that he could get it, right now—this man, she didn't know.

But she wanted to know him. She couldn't stop herself from wanting to know everything about him.

Drawing deep down inside herself, looking for courage, she eased forward across the abyss of doubts and fears, across the mere inches that separated them until they were almost touching.

She waited there in full surrender while his arms moved ever so slowly to settle her into a tender embrace. One hand settled her body against the strength of his while another pressed her head against his shoulder.

She breathed in the scent of him, felt the warmth of him, the strength and gentleness and patience—she'd never known patience from him.

One of his hands made small circles against her back and the other one was caught up in her hair, a soothing touch, a loving touch.

She let herself melt against him, gave herself up to the comfort and the reassurance he was offering.

They stayed there for a long time. She lost all track of time, lost a little of her fear of him, but none of the longing she had for him. It had only grown stronger.

His hands were running over her body then, over her arms and her shoulders, her back and finally her hips. With the slightest pressure, he eased her lower body against his.

She gasped as she felt his arousal pulsing between them, but she wasn't afraid of his passion anymore.

He was going to give her time to get used to this, a gift that she'd never expected from him.

He kissed her once, slowly, sweetly, thoroughly, and set her to trembling. If her legs could barely hold her, it didn't matter because he was holding her. He wasn't going to let go.

He ended the kiss, but stayed close, with his lips just a breath away.

"Give me another chance, Rebecca."

She would have given him almost anything right then. She chose to give him her honesty.

"I'm still afraid."

"So am I, but then there's nothing new about that. You've always scared me to death."

She doubted that. He'd never been afraid of anything—not until that first night he'd come to see Sammy, at least. She would have pondered over the idea of Tucker actually being afraid of her, but he kissed her again. He kissed her like a man who had all the time in the world and wanted to do nothing but kiss her, and she gloried in it.

"Just a chance," he whispered against her lips. "Give me that."

"All right," she said, a moment before his lips took hers again.

*   *   *

It was too hot to sleep that night, and Rebecca stayed awake long after he left.

She hadn't forgotten anything about the years she and Tucker had spent together. It would have been so much easier if she had, but the memories were still there.

Except, things were changing.

The pain was still there, though not as immense or as hurtful now that so much time had passed. It was getting harder to hold on to her memories of the bad times. The past was fading, and the present seemed so much more important.

At times, he was so much like the man she married—gorgeous, charming, full of flattery, so sure of himself. And then at other times, she saw a new maturity in him, a sense of purpose and of responsibility, a vulnerability and a determination to make things right between him and Sammy.

She wasn't worried about him and Sammy anymore. They were wonderful together, happy just to be together. And she believed that they would always be together now, which meant that she and Tucker were going to have some kind of relationship.

A chance? he'd asked. Just a chance.

She drew the green silk robe closer to her, missing Tucker's own special brand of warmth, despite the heat of the night.

She'd agreed to give him a chance.

A part of her still wanted him, in a way she'd wanted no other man in all the time they'd been apart. A part of her was still terrified of being hurt again.

Now that he wasn't holding her in his arms, setting her blood to boiling, she wondered whether her fear or her desire would prevail.

Chapter 12

Three days later Rebecca hung up the phone and just stood there, staring at the man who'd so completely thrown her off balance, once again. This was becoming her normal state of mind when Tucker was around, and she didn't care for it.

"I guess you just found out where I'm living," Tucker said.

"No, I just heard about where you worked in Louisiana."

He gave her a wicked grin, one that the devil himself would have been proud of. Tucker enjoyed throwing her off balance, always had.

"Surprised you, didn't I?"

"Yes," she said, growing more and more uneasy.

He'd been working for the state of Louisiana for the last three years, most of it as chief counsel to a special commission set up to try to take on the petrochemical industry in the state—something that was a nearly impossible task in Louisiana.

But according to a friend with the Sierra Club in Baton Rouge, Tucker had done an incredible job. He'd taken on some issues that had been seen as hopeless and had actually won a few rounds.

Rebecca simply couldn't believe it.

She'd believed that Tucker took the job here in Tallahassee because he wanted to be near her and Sammy, but now she found out that he'd been doing similar work for the past three years. It just didn't make any sense.

Unless he really had changed, in more ways than she'd thought possible.

She stared at him, wishing she could see right into his soul, the way he seemed to be able to see into hers. But she couldn't. She couldn't begin to understand him.

"Why didn't you tell me?" she asked.

He shook his head, as if he didn't understand himself.

"Would you have believed me?" he said finally.

"Probably not."

"And even if you had believed me, I didn't think it would have mattered, not at first." His arms slipped around her waist and he moved a step closer. "I hope it matters now."

After the other night.

He didn't say it, but he was thinking it.

She hadn't seen him in three days, and she'd been bracing herself for the meeting.

Rebecca was uneasy about seeing him. Their relationship had changed; she'd agreed to give him another chance. But she wasn't sure what that meant or how it would work or what he would expect from her now.

How did a woman go about getting to know a man all over again after she'd been married to him, had a child with him and divorced him?

She stared up at him and felt this awful push and pull inside herself, felt herself swaying toward him, wanting him, coming alive in his presence, yet at the same time wanting to run from him, from the fear of being hurt again by him.

What in the world was she going to do with him?

"I can't see you leaving private practice to go to work for the state."

He smiled, sly as a fox, and she had a feeling she'd just walked right into his trap.

"You mean you can't see the man you *used* to know leaving private practice to go to work for the state."

She was silent. That was the essence of it. That's where the confusion came in—because the man standing before her was the same man who'd hurt her so badly before, and yet he wasn't.

"Hey—" he tilted her face up to his "—it's all right, Rebecca. We've got time. We've got all the time in the world."

"All right." She welcomed his patience, but wondered how long it would hold out. "So where are you living?"

"Your parents—at the guest house."

"Guest house? You mean the apartment above the garage?"

He nodded, clearly amused.

"It's a dump."

"No it's not. Nobody's been in it for years, so it was a little dusty. It needed a good cleaning and a paint job, but it's fine."

He'd left her stunned, again. Guest house was a kind description at best from what she remembered about the place. When she'd been growing up, the housekeeper and her husband, who tended the grounds, had lived in the apartment above the three-car garage.

He was going to live in the old servants' quarters?

"Why would you want to live there?"

"It's available. It's not far from the office. It's not far from you and Sammy, and I'm tired of looking for a place."

"Still... It's not—" Not what she would have expected from him? It seemed nothing was as she'd expected it to be. "That's really all?"

He shrugged again. "I need to get to work. The job's been empty for months now, and the work's piled up. When things calm down, I'll find a place."

"Now—" he kissed her on the nose, then consulted the clock on the mantel "—how much time do we have before the torture session begins?"

That's how they'd come to refer to the soccer games—sheer torture. She couldn't understand why Sammy put himself through it, or why she couldn't talk him out of giving it up. But he was determined, and when he set his mind to it, he could be as stubborn as Tucker.

Sammy didn't freeze up on the field anymore, but he didn't play well, either. He was scared of the ball, and in a sport where the object was to get the ball and kick it into the other team's goal, Sammy played with one objective in mind—to stay as far away from the ball as possible.

She looked at the clock and groaned. "Game starts in twenty minutes. We need to go."

"I guess we couldn't be late deliberately? Maybe we could miss the game all together? Do Sammy a favor."

She was tempted, very tempted.

"Why don't you think about it for a minute or two," Tucker said as his lips came down to meet hers.

He was holding her lightly. He moved slowly, and she had more than enough time to pull away, if she wanted to.

She considered it, but found herself standing there, watching his lips come closer and closer, feeling a shiver of anticipation work its way up her spine. She wanted him to kiss her. She didn't even try to deny it, not anymore. Just a kiss, she told herself as her lips opened beneath his. She could handle that.

Another kiss.

Another chance.

She gave herself up to his long, leisurely exploration of her mouth and pushed her memories of the past one step further behind her.

Sammy came in from the backyard and caught them kissing in the hallway.

They broke apart at the sound of the French door closing and found the boy staring up at them with an incredibly serious look on his face.

No one said a word, but Rebecca's face turned crimson as she backed away from Tucker.

"Try not to look so guilty," Tucker said in a voice too soft for Sammy to hear. "It was just a kiss." Then he turned to his son, ruffled his hair and said, "Hey, sport. Ready for the game?"

"Uh-huh."

And then Sammy stared at them some more.

"I'm going to change before we leave," Rebecca said and fled down the hall and up the stairs.

"So—" Tucker looked down at his puzzled child "—we need to get going, Sammy. Are you ready?"

"Uh-huh." He nodded, then paused. "Jimmy Horton says kissing is gross."

Tucker smiled. You could always count on Jimmy Horton to have an opinion about everything. "Oh, he does, does he?"

"Uh-huh. But he says grown-ups do it, anyway."

"Well, Sammy, you remember when we talked about this. Jimmy Horton's only seven years old. He doesn't know everything. Remember?"

"Uh-huh. But—" Sammy hesitated and started scuffing his shoes, one against the other, something he did a good bit from the looks of the sneakers.

His tentativeness still worried Tucker, and it tugged on his heartstrings at the same time. He wanted to wrap Sammy up in his arms and protect him from the whole world so no one would ever frighten him or hurt his feelings again. If only Dads could do that...

"It's okay, sport. Go ahead. You can ask me anything."

"Well," Sammy still stared at the floor. "If Mom's kissing you and all that stuff, maybe she's not mad at you anymore."

Tucker got down on Sammy's level and wondered how a more experienced father would handle this. He was still running blind with so much of this parenting stuff, and he wondered if he'd ever be at ease in the situation. He figured it had to get easier with experience, although everyone he asked about it said that wasn't so. Most parents said it never got easier.

Of course, most parents hadn't disappeared from their children's lives for the better part of six years.

Tucker guessed he'd have to do what he'd been doing all along—follow the best advice another attorney in his old office had given him about dealing with children's questions—keep it simple and be honest with them.

But nothing about this situation was simple. Hell, Tucker didn't even understand it himself. How could he hope to explain it to a six-year-old?

Sammy looked up at him with so much trust in his eyes that it still amazed him. He couldn't disappoint him, and he couldn't allow his little boy to be hurt again, no matter what the cost.

Tucker gathered his thoughts and took his best shot.

"Sammy, it's just not as simple as your mom not being mad anymore. Remember when we talked about it before? I can't just say I'm sorry and expect your mom to forgive me. Sometimes the things you've done to somebody are just too big and too important, and saying you're sorry just isn't enough. Remember?"

Sammy nodded. "But Jimmy Horton's dad left, and then he came back so—"

So when are you coming back home, Dad? He could hear the question Sammy wanted to ask.

Soon, he wanted to tell Sammy. He prayed to God that it would be soon.

He wanted to come home. *Wanted* didn't even begin to explain the intensity of his longing.

Strange how for years when he'd had no idea of what he really needed, he'd been able to get anything that he wanted. But now, when he'd finally figured out exactly what he needed—Rebecca and Sammy—he didn't have a clue as to how to go about getting them back.

He was running blind again, running on nothing but his yearning for them and his determination not to give up, not ever.

"Sammy," he said finally, then halted in mid-sentence. Rebecca was standing in the hallway behind them with a stricken look on her face and with tears glittering in her eyes.

Damn, he cursed inwardly, knowing that one of the biggest obstacles standing in their way was the idea that Sammy might get hurt. If they tried to patch things up— if they let Sammy get his hopes up that the three of them might become a family again—and it didn't work out, Sammy would be hurt all over again.

He knew that. He worried about it, too, but there was nothing in this world that was going to make him back away from her now without doing his damnedest to get her back.

He just had to make sure Sammy didn't get hurt in the process.

"Sammy," he said, turning his attention back to the boy, "I'm not Jimmy Horton's dad. And you can't think that just because your mother lets me kiss her that we're going to get back together. Okay?"

"'Kay"

"But the important thing for you to remember is that whether or not your mother and I ever get back together again, we'll always be here for you. Do you understand that?"

A very serious Sammy nodded. "Yes."

"We'll always love you, and we'll always be around to take care of you. Okay?"

"'Kay."

In the background Rebecca smiled at him through her tears. It was an agreement they'd already come to themselves. They would not yell or scream or fight in front of Sammy, and they wouldn't fight over him. They wouldn't

make him any more a victim of their failed marriage than
he already was.

Tucker thought about pulling Sammy to him and
holding him close, for a long time. He wished he could
just hold them both, but figured he'd better not push his
luck.

Patience, he reminded himself. They were together, for
now, and they had time.

He settled for ruffling Sammy's hair, and won a smile
from his son for that. Tucker wasn't sure he'd gotten
through to the boy, but he didn't know what else to say.
So he let it drop for the moment.

"Come on," he said to Sammy. "Let's get on the road.
We wouldn't want to miss this game."

He winked at Rebecca as he said it, and she rolled her
eyes at him, but she smiled, too.

It would be torture for sure. All the other boys would
run after the ball, and Sammy, as slyly as possible, would
run away from it.

Tucker would sit in the stands and hold Rebecca's
hand. As long as none of the other kids made fun of
Sammy, they would consider themselves lucky. And they
would pray for the end of soccer season.

Rebecca hid in the kitchen of Tucker's new apartment, where she couldn't help but overhear his ongoing
argument with his mother.

At least from here she didn't have to watch it, as well.

It was Tuesday afternoon, moving day for Tucker.
Sammy wanted to help, so Rebecca agreed to let him take
the bus to her parents' house after school.

She still couldn't understand why Tucker would want
to live there, and her curiosity got the better of her. She
went over as well—a decision she quickly came to regret.

Tucker's mother was there, and she couldn't understand her son's choice of living quarters, either. So far, no amount of explaining would satisfy her.

That wouldn't have been so bad, if Tucker's father hadn't chosen to make a rare appearance, as well.

Clearly his mother and father hated each other.

Rebecca had fled to the kitchen where she started unpacking boxes and washing things before she put them away. The noise coming from the living room had quietened a little since Tucker had sent his father and Sammy out to pick up some take-out food for dinner.

"Divide and conquer," he'd explained to Rebecca a few minutes ago as he hauled in a box of kitchen things for her to unload. "It's the only way to handle my parents. Together, they're impossible."

From what she'd seen today, she tended to agree. The air was thick with that and a constant backbiting that seemed to sting everyone in the room but them. They were oblivious to it.

She was sure this wasn't one of the worst arguments they'd ever had.

Tucker's mother started it when she told him that since she and her second husband had returned home to Tallahassee from their summer house in Vermont, they'd decided to go farther south for the winter. The Caribbean, maybe, or perhaps Mexico. There was no reason Tucker couldn't stay at their house for as long as he needed it, she said.

Nonsense, said his father. No need for him to worry about settling into anyone else's house when a friend of his father's owned rental property all over town. He was sure he could find Tucker something infinitely more suitable than what he had now or what he would find at his mother's.

It went on and on, back and forth, angry strikes at each other masked as an offer to help their son. They didn't look at each other, and they hardly directed any words at each other. They talked through Tucker; they struck out at each other through him.

Rebecca had hated for Sammy even to hear as much of the argument as he had. Her child, hers and Tuckers, had never been exposed to the kind of bitterness that must have been an integral part of Tucker's childhood.

Tucker sidestepped his parents' questions at first. He ignored them and kept hauling in boxes. When he looked ready to murder someone, he sent his father and Sammy out to find some food.

With Tucker's father gone now, his mother continued to press her case.

It seemed that his parents were determined to make Tucker choose between the two of them, something he refused to do.

Rebecca was beginning to see why the place above the garage hadn't looked so bad to him.

She watched him and wondered if things had always been this way between them and why she hadn't noticed it before. Of course, she and Tucker hadn't spent much time with his parents. They'd been around for the wedding, of course, but she'd been so caught up in Tucker, she'd barely known her own name at the time. But still— this kind of acrimony was practically impossible to miss.

"Has it always been this way?" she asked him quietly when he hauled in another box.

"No." He smiled despite everything and kissed her forehead. "It used to be worse. They used to hate each other even more. And when I was a child, I couldn't get out of their way as easily as I can now."

He said it lightly, and she saw a remnant of the happy-go-lucky man she'd married. But the whole thing had to hurt him. It had to.

"Do they always have to outdo each other?"

She knew about this tendency well. Ever since his parents had rediscovered their grandson, they'd showered him with presents. Rebecca's house wouldn't hold any more, and when she couldn't talk them out of sending more, she'd started taking the toys to one of the homeless shelters downtown.

All those presents, yet they'd found little time to spend with Sammy. Didn't they know that things couldn't make up for just a little of their time?

"Not always," Tucker said on his way back outside for more boxes. "My father wasn't that fond of paying child support after they split, and for the first few years, my mother couldn't match anything my father gave me. But that didn't stop them. My mother made a wonderful martyr."

Rebecca could easily imagine his mother the martyr, but the idea that she and Tucker had struggled to make ends meet was a surprise. Tucker's father was a well-to-do man, and for as long as she'd known his mother, the woman had been married to a man who owned a department-store chain.

Of course, it probably explained why Tucker had insisted on paying alimony when they'd divorced. When Rebecca had refused to accept it, he'd settled for paying a ridiculously large child-support payment, instead, no doubt thinking that it would be enough to support an ex-wife as well as a child.

Tucker wouldn't be very happy to know that Rebecca hadn't touched the money in years. It was accumulating in a mutual fund account for Sammy, whose net worth was definitely much higher than his mother's.

Rebecca stayed in the kitchen and tried not to listen to the rest of it. Finally his mother left.

Tucker stayed in the living room, staring at the boxes. He'd forgotten how bad it could get between his mother and his father. He hadn't had the misfortune to be in the same room with them for years; he knew better than to put himself in that position.

He scowled. There was a fine tremor to his hands that he didn't care for, yet couldn't seem to control. You'd think a grown man wouldn't let his parents get to him this way.

He heard footsteps behind him, then remembered that Rebecca was still here, that she must have heard the whole thing. Then he felt her hand on his back.

"I don't know how you stood it," she said.

He stiffened. "Don't pity me, Rebecca. It's the last thing I want from you."

Her hand stayed there, pressed against his back, stroking up and down in a soothing motion. It was the first time he could remember since his return that she'd reached out and touched him first.

"It's not pity," she said. "I'm just worried about you. And I'm wondering how I missed seeing all this animosity while we were married."

"I didn't want you to see it," he said. It had been a closely guarded secret of his, because his parents embodied the things he'd feared most for his relationship with her.

If he'd been a stronger man, he would have walked away from her years ago. He would have known that he would have been much safer with someone else, anyone else, as long as he didn't need them as much as he needed Rebecca.

"I'm sorry." He closed his eyes. "I didn't mean to snap at you."

"It's all right."

She put her arms around him from behind and leaned her head against his shoulder. God, it felt good to have her touch him like this, no matter what the reason.

"Tucker? Did you really think we'd end up like them? That we'd hate each other just as much? That we'd make Sammy as miserable as you must have been?"

"Maybe."

He wished she'd just drop it. He wished she hadn't seen what she had seen. He wished she'd just hold on to him for a while and let him believe that in the end, she was going to be his again.

"Is that why, Tucker? I need to know."

He searched for the right words. He tried to remember that crazy, mixed-up time in their lives. And he had to be honest with her. He'd made a promise to himself and would make one to her when she was ready to hear it. He was going to be absolutely honest with her.

"When it came right down to it, Rebecca, I just couldn't take that risk."

She held him, still, and he breathed a little easier now that he'd told her. Maybe she would understand someday. Maybe she could forgive him. And then they could start over.

"Do you believe me?"

She was a long time answering, and he wished he hadn't pushed the issue.

"It's just that— It's so hard for me to imagine you being afraid of anything. I thought I was the only one who was scared."

"Oh, Rebecca." He turned around and held her lightly, at arm's length so he look down at her beautiful face. "You scared me to death. You always have."

He couldn't have surprised her more; that was evident from the look on her face.

"I couldn't get you out of my mind. I couldn't have you. I couldn't walk away from you. I knew you were so young, so inexperienced, and I knew that it would have to be marriage or nothing with you."

She lowered her head, and her lashes fanned down over her green eyes, shielding them from his gaze.

He held her as he continued. "I didn't want to get married because I knew how it could end up and I didn't want to take that risk. But in the end, I couldn't walk away, either."

"And now?" she said, without looking at him.

Tucker smiled and tilted her chin up. "I can't live the rest of my life without you. Sometimes I don't think I can make it another day."

She looked frightened by that—not the reaction he'd been hoping for.

He held her, anyway. He wished, for a moment, that he'd never promised to take things slowly between them, that he could haul her into his arms, carry her to his bed and make love to her until dawn.

They'd always tried to overcome their anger and their fears with their passion; it had worked, but not for long.

It wouldn't work now. He knew that.

So he just held her and waited. He would wait for the day when she wasn't afraid anymore, for the day when she decided that she could trust him, just a little.

The day would come. He believed that. He had to believe it.

* * *

They unpacked, ate some of a half-warm pizza that Tucker's father and Sammy brought back, then Tucker's father left.

Rebecca and Sammy were getting ready to leave, too, when she heard Tucker's stomach growl, then laughed. It hadn't been the greatest dinner in the world, and they hadn't eaten that much of it.

She took pity on him, here in this empty apartment with the empty kitchen, and invited him back to the house for whatever they could find in her freezer. But they didn't quite make it to the kitchen. They arrived at her house and found a little boy on the front porch, instead.

The infamous Jimmy Horton, trouble incarnate, huddled in the darkened corner of the porch, looking angry and defiant, all at the same time.

Chapter 13

Jimmy Horton wouldn't tell them anything, except that he'd been on their porch for a while and his mother didn't know where he was.

Rebecca finally gave up trying to get anything out of him. She gave Sammy and Jimmy some homemade chocolate caramel brownies and milk, then sent the boys upstairs so she could call Mrs. Horton. Ten minutes later, she finally managed to get through to the boy's frantic mother, who'd been on the phone calling everyone she knew to try to locate Jimmy.

Rebecca reassured the woman that her son was safe, though clearly upset about something. And then Rebecca found out why.

"What is it?" Tucker asked. He was beside her in an instant.

"Damn!" she said softly as she hung up the phone. "We're in trouble."

"What?"

"Jimmy Horton's dad moved out again, for good this time, his mother says."

Tucker cursed, more harshly than she had.

"Sammy's not going to take this well."

"No," he said. "And it's no telling what kind of crap that kid's telling him now."

Their eyes met and held. Jimmy Horton was right up there with God as far as Sammy was concerned; they both knew that. Sammy believed every word the kid said.

"Come on," Tucker said. "We've got to get him away from Sammy."

They headed for the stairs, but knew they were too late when they walked into Sammy's bedroom.

Both boys turned tear-filled eyes on Tucker. Jimmy Horton glared defiantly at him. Sammy, with his lower lip trembling and tear tracks on his face, looked like he'd lost his best friend in the world.

"He will," Jimmy Horton said, glaring at Tucker.

"He won't," Sammy said, though he didn't sound nearly as certain.

"Will, too." Jimmy retorted.

Tucker felt sorry for the poor, mixed-up kid, but still could have strangled him right then and there.

"I will what?" he said, bracing himself for the answer.

Jimmy Horton faltered for a moment and looked as if he might start crying again, but he didn't. He just got mad all over again.

"You'll leave, too," Jimmy insisted. "Just like my dad."

Tucker watched Sammy's face the whole time. He was confused and vulnerable. Their whole relationship was so vulnerable at this stage.

Tucker knew that Sammy liked him, enjoyed spending time with him, but his son just didn't know him that well. The bond between them was still so fragile. The trust hadn't had the time it needed to take root.

So Tucker wasn't that surprised when he looked into his son's eyes and saw nothing but doubts and fears.

He sighed heavily, wishing he could curse some more. He raged inside at the unfairness of it all. He was ready to pay for his own sins, but he didn't need to carry the burden for Jimmy Horton's dad, as well.

Rebecca slipped her hand into his and gave him a reassuring squeeze that steadied him a little.

Tucker held on tight, but didn't turn around to look at her. He didn't want to see the doubts in her eyes, too.

Her trust in him was tenuous, at best.

"I'm not going anywhere," he told Sammy. But the boy's only response was to stare at the floor.

Tucker felt as if everything he'd worked for in the past four months was slipping away—at least he did until Rebecca squeezed his hand again.

God, he wanted this woman back. He wanted his son. He wanted them to be a family.

Rebecca slipped an arm around his waist from behind, and her touch settled him.

"Come on, Jimmy," she said. "Your mother's worried about you, and she's coming to get you."

Jimmy shot her a defiant look, but got to his feet, anyway. The boy's eyes were red from crying, and he was so angry he was shaking.

So this is what it looked like when a father left his son, Tucker thought.

He wasn't ever going to leave his son again. Now, if he could only find the words to make Sammy believe it.

Tucker stood in the doorway and waited after Rebecca and Jimmy left the room. Sammy didn't say a word. He just sat on the floor beside his bed and looked out the window, and every now and then he gave a sniffle.

Tucker dreaded this conversation. He was fighting for his life here, because he knew now that life wasn't worth a hill of beans to him without Sammy and Rebecca. And he just didn't know what to say.

"Sammy?"

Nothing. No response from the child sitting on the floor.

Tucker got down on the floor with Sammy, right in front of him.

Still nothing.

Tucker cleared his throat and searched for a beginning.

"It's too bad about Jimmy's dad," he said finally.

Sammy gave a barely discernible nod.

They were making progress.

"What did he tell you, Sammy?"

Sammy backhanded his nose and sniffled again. "His dad left again."

"Yes." Tucker eased closer, aching to take his son in his arms.

"And Jimmy said he's not coming back, not ever."

"Sammy?" Tucker scooted over so his back was against the bed and he was right beside his son. "You're not Jimmy Horton, and I'm not his dad. Just because Jimmy's dad left, doesn't mean that—"

"He said you'd go, too." Sammy said, sobbing. "Jimmy knows, 'cause it's the same thing that happened to him, 'n' now it's gonna happen to me."

"No, it's not." Tucker couldn't stand it anymore. He hauled Sammy onto his lap and pulled him close. "I'm not going anywhere, Sammy. I swear it."

Sammy sobbed pitifully, like a little, lost puppy. He shook and shivered with each gasp for breath and buried his head against Tucker's shoulder.

They stayed that way for a long time.

"I'm not going away," he whispered over and over again, as he rocked back and forth and smoothed down Sammy's hair.

Tucker wasn't going to give up, and he wasn't going to go away, not ever again. He was going to be here for his son, and he was going to teach his wife to trust him again, to love him again, or he'd die trying.

Tucker held his son a little tighter, until Sammy's sobs subsided and his skinny little arms came around Tucker's middle.

Sammy snuggled against his chest and settled down.

"I don't wantcha to go," he muttered into Tucker's shirt, and the big lump in his throat that had been threatening to choke him all night finally started to shrink a little.

"Good," Tucker said and kissed Sammy's head. "Because I'm not."

Sammy leaned forward and rubbed his eyes, then wiped his hands on his shirt before settling in against Tucker's chest again. "I missed ya, before, when you were gone, all the time," he admitted.

"I missed you, too, Sammy."

"Do ya think . . ."

"What?"

Sammy considered for a minute, choosing his words carefully. "That me and you and Mom'll ever be all together again, like when I was a little baby?"

Tucker froze.

At the doorway to Sammy's bedroom, Rebecca clamped a hand over her mouth, but not soon enough to stop the gasp that alerted Tucker to her presence.

His eyes met her tear-filled ones in a shared moment of anguish. Everything they'd done in the past, every mistake they'd made, all the regrets they had, seemed to have come together in this one, heart-wrenching moment.

Tucker looked to Rebecca to guide him, to answer Sammy's question, to answer all the questions he hadn't yet asked her, because he didn't think she was ready to hear them.

But Sammy had asked them for him.

Is there a chance for us? he asked without words. Can we put it back together again?

A frightened Rebecca shook her head no as her tears started to fall.

Yes. He mouthed the word over Sammy's head and then waited, daring her to contradict him.

She dared. Slowly, sadly, she shook her head no.

It only made him more determined than ever.

She was scared.

Sammy was scared.

Hell, he was scared, too, but that didn't bother him anymore, because he finally felt alive again.

Alive and scared beat the hell out of alone and empty any day.

And he wasn't going anywhere.

"Yes," he whispered, too softly for Sammy to hear. But Rebecca knew what he said. She read the word on his lips.

Rebecca wrapped her arms around her middle and blinked hard. Tears glistened in her eyes, mingling there with the fear.

She was still so afraid.

"Will we, Daddy?" Sammy said.

Tucker squeezed Sammy to him. He closed his eyes and absorbed the warmth that flooded through him every time he heard the word "Daddy" on his son's lips.

"Sammy, even if we all never live together, we'll still be here for you. You'll always have your mother, and you'll always have me. And we'll always love you, all right?"

"Uh-huh, but do you think we'll ever all live together again?"

Tucker listened to his heart. He refused to make a promise that he couldn't keep, but he could tell Sammy what was in his heart.

"I hope so, Sammy. More than anything else in the world, I hope so."

Sammy smiled for the first time since Jimmy Horton had shown up.

When Tucker looked up at the doorway again, Rebecca was gone.

Sammy finally settled down, and Tucker went to find Rebecca.

She was on the back deck, in the dark, save for the starlight above. And she was near the breaking point, though still trying to muster her defenses against him.

He could tell that by the way she held herself, arms wrapped around her middle and shoulders hunched up and inward, as if that could hold all her feelings inside. He could tell by the way she took two steps backward for every one step forward that he took. No big surprise there. They'd been doing that ever since he returned.

But he kept moving forward because before too long, she was going to run out of room to back away any farther.

Tucker waited there beside her, staring up into the heavens. If he'd been a religious man, he'd be praying for all he was worth right now.

"What did you tell him?" she said, breaking the silence that had enveloped him.

"That I loved him. That you loved him. That we always would."

"Good. That was good."

She didn't look at him when she spoke. She looked at the stars.

"Sammy said…" Tucker's voice broke and he tried to cover by clearing his throat. "He told me that he loved me, too."

"He does, and that's what matters. Not you and me or—"

"We matter, Rebecca. It means a hell of a lot to me, and I think it means just as much to you."

"I can't, Tucker." She bent her head and covered her eyes with her hand. "I just can't."

"You can," he insisted. "You still have feelings for me. Tell me that you don't. I dare you."

Her head came up and her arms went back around her waist, tighter than before, as if she were trying to pull inside herself. "It's just too much. It's too hard. The risks are too—"

"I want you back, Rebecca." The words burst out from him. He couldn't stand to hold them in any longer. "I haven't said it before, because I didn't think you were ready to hear them, but I can't wait any longer."

Rebecca cringed. The pain she felt at his words was like a brand, searing its way into her heart.

Wanted, he'd said. Not loved.

There'd been a time when she would have given anything—anything—to have heard him say that he loved her, and another time when she would have settled for simply feeling as if he still wanted her.

That's the way it had been between them before.

He'd wanted. She'd loved.

He'd walked away. She'd shattered into a million little pieces.

He'd hardly said he loved her, even when they'd been married, and she'd known it hadn't been love that had moved him to marry her. It had been his need for her—desire coupled with something deeper, something more mysterious, something almost spiritual.

He'd needed her then, but not for long. And she wouldn't be able to bear it when at some point in the future he decided once again that he didn't need her anymore.

"Say something, Rebecca. Say anything."

"I don't know what to say."

She felt his arms come around her from behind, felt his warmth and his strength. He moved slowly, giving her time to object. He held her gently, and she could have easily gotten away from him, if she'd wanted to do that.

"Tell me you don't feel anything for me anymore," he whispered, his breath fanning her right ear and sending a shiver down her spine.

"I don't love you anymore, Tucker. I stopped a long time ago."

He went absolutely still behind her, but he didn't let go. So she forced herself to continue.

"And I don't want you anymore."

"That's a lie," he said, dangerously quiet and still. "Maybe you don't want to want me, but you do."

"It's the past," she said quickly, before she lost the courage to go on. "If we could go back to when we first met. If you'd been like this then. If you'd wanted to be a father to Sammy, and if I'd been ready to be a wife—"

Her voice broke on a sob, and he held her tighter. Finally, she let her head fall back against his shoulder and let the misery consume her.

She'd played through the "what ifs" so many times in her mind. But the worst one to deal with was—what if they were meeting now for the first time? What if he had changed and she had grown and had more confidence in herself? Where would they be headed now if they were meeting for the first time?

She let her mind wander while he held her in his arms. They'd be together now, if they could wipe out the past and start again. The only thing standing between them was her fears that he'd hurt her again the way he had before.

"Oh, Tucker."

"We can't go back," he said, clearly frustrated. "Don't you think I would if I could? Don't you know that I'd give anything—anything in this world—if I could change things, if I could somehow take away the hurt and erase all the mistakes."

He turned her to face him, tilted her head up so that he could look into her eyes.

"I'd give anything, Rebecca."

She saw the pain in his beautiful brown eyes, a pain so deep that it was hard to watch it there.

This man, whom she thought felt no pain and harbored no regrets, had paid the price for his mistakes and for some of hers, as well.

"We can't go back," he said. "But we have a lifetime ahead of us, Rebecca. I don't want to be alone anymore. I don't want to spend another minute without you."

And then his lips came down to hers, surprising her, catching her in his spell before she even had time to protest, as if she would have had the strength to protest.

"Come to bed with me, Rebecca." He whispered it against her lips.

"Tucker?" It was the last thing in the world she expected from him then.

"You want to know if there's anything left between us. You want to know if it would still feel the way it used to. If it's still as good as it used to be. If you'll still feel like you belong to me.

"Come upstairs with me. Show me I'm wrong. Show me you don't want me anymore. I'll show you I'm right." And then he turned and walked away. One scorching look at her, and he was gone, into the house.

She walked after him to say...something. She didn't know what. But all she did was watch him go up the stairs.

To her bedroom!

She couldn't believe he was just going up to her bedroom, like a man who had every right to be there. And she couldn't believe that once again, he'd looked inside her and saw just what she'd been wondering.

Would it feel just the same?

It couldn't.

Would the feelings still be there with him? The ones she thought she'd lost forever? The ones she'd never felt with another man?

Or had that part of her just shriveled up and died? That's how it had felt before he came back—it felt like something inside her had just died.

She was too chicken to find out. That was part of it. But most of all, her sense of self-preservation was too strong.

"Tucker?" she said as she stormed into her own bedroom. "This is ridic—"

And then she started tripping over her own words until she decided that the safest thing to do would be to close her mouth.

He was undressing. He was in her bedroom taking off his clothes. His shirt was gone. His socks and shoes, too. She'd come into the room just in time to hear the rasp of a zipper and then the sound of his pants falling into a heap on the floor.

Her mouth went dry, and she turned to look away as he stripped away his last remaining piece of clothing. At least she tried to look away. God, he was the most beautiful man.

And he was climbing into her bed.

Chapter 14

He waited.

He was getting better at this waiting stuff. And it was getting easier to wait, because it was the best way he knew to throw her off balance.

That and climbing naked into her bed. That seemed to have worked especially well.

So he waited. And remembered.

There'd been a time, shortly after their marriage, when Rebecca had been a little shy. She'd hesitated about coming to bed with him. He used to sit in bed, naked, just like this, and watch her while she got ready for bed. He watched while she lingered in the bathroom, then at her dressing table, brushing her hair, then finally undressing slowly.

It had irritated him a little, at first, to see her reluctance, to know that for some reason she was still a little uncomfortable with that most intimate side of their marriage.

Not that she hadn't pleased him. She had. And he had pleased her. There'd been no doubt about that.

But he'd pushed her, too far, too fast. He'd overwhelmed her a little with a passion that had frightened her at first. He'd wanted everything from her, all of her, with no reservations. And she'd seemed determined to hold something back from him.

And then he'd finally figured it out. What he'd taken for reluctance hadn't been that at all. She was just a little shy. She was searching for some measure of control in the middle of the whirlwind that had overtaken them.

When he'd finally backed off, just a little, and given her some time to get used to things, she'd been fine. She'd come to him in her own time.

She would come tonight, on her own.

If he'd pushed, he could have gotten her here already, but he didn't want it to happen that way. He wanted her to come to him, and then maybe she wouldn't regret it in the morning.

Maybe, if there were no regrets about the night, they could start planning their future.

Together.

In the morning.

"Come to bed, Rebecca," he said finally.

She was speechless. Her cheeks were flushed, her heart pounding, her thoughts all a jumble, and she couldn't have pried her eyes away from the man in her bed for anything.

The naked man in her bed who was calmly inviting her to join him.

"Tucker, this is crazy."

"It makes perfect sense," he said, warming her whole body with nothing but the look in his eyes and the sight of him there in her bed. "You say you don't love me anymore. You claim you don't want me anymore, but your body tells me something else, Rebecca Jane.

"Come over here and show me you don't want me," he said, turning back the covers in invitation.

"Stop it," she said, scrambling over to the bed and catching the edge of the comforter before he uncovered any more of himself.

He tugged back, just enough so that she ended up sitting on the bed beside him.

And then he smiled, wickedly.

"Show me," he said. "Show me you don't want me, Rebecca."

She sat there, trying to avoid his eyes, trying not to stare at the subtle play of the muscles in his chest as he inhaled and exhaled.

She'd never known the act of breathing could be so sexy.

And she knew just how all those muscles felt, just how she fit against them, how they fit together.

She remembered the very first time he'd taken her blouse and her camisole off and held her close, her breasts nestled in the little golden hairs that curled tight against his chest.

The sensations—she couldn't even describe them, except to say that he'd opened up a whole new world to her, a sensual, breathtaking world.

And, God help her, she still wondered if he could take her there.

She gave a start when his hand closed over hers. He must have caught her staring at his chest, must have read her mind, once again, because he took her hand and put it over his heart, held it there so she could feel the rise and fall as his lungs filled and emptied.

"Come and show me," he said, his heart pounding beneath her hand. "Show me you feel nothing for me."

She pulled her hand away as if she'd been scalded by his touch, by his tormenting.

She couldn't do that. And he knew it.

Rebecca could barely breathe now, and her voice trembled with something—fear and yearning—that all-too familiar tangle of emotions that he'd always managed to bring to the surface in her.

Yes and no.

Stop, but don't stop.

Make love to me, but don't make me love you. Not again.

Why didn't he just put an end to it? she thought. He would win out in the end. He always did with her.

Why didn't he just pull her into his arms and trap her there on the bed underneath him? She didn't have it in her to protest anymore, and he knew it.

She braced herself as best she could, and looked at him as he sat there in the bed waiting for her.

He knew that she'd give in. He'd known it all along, just as he knew how much she wanted him, yet didn't.

If she'd been stronger, she would have kicked him out of the house by now. She never would have let him get this close, never would have let him see that this attraction between them was still there.

If only she'd been stronger.

But she wasn't that strong when it came to him. She didn't have the ability to hide her feelings from him. And she couldn't walk away from him. Not now. Not anymore.

All she could do was hope that being with him again wouldn't be anything like she remembered.

She could hope that maybe she'd prove to him, to herself as well, that the passion had died out along with the love she once felt for him.

She didn't love him anymore.

She said it to herself, for herself this time and not in some deliberate, desperate attempt to hurt him, as she'd done before downstairs.

She couldn't love him anymore.

Maybe this would prove it.

Maybe it would lay to rest all the ghosts of the past and all their hopes that they could somehow put their tangled lives back together again.

And if it did that, it was a small price to pay as she saw it.

Rebecca looked down at him, there in her bed, the sheet riding dangerously low on his belly, those little curls of hair trailing down the center of his chest, down under the sheet.

And then she started trembling all over again.

"What do you want from me, Tucker?"

"Tonight. Just give me one night, all right?"

She couldn't breathe, couldn't speak, though she managed to nod.

Yes.

The tension in the room soared instantly.

He smiled, tried to hold it back, but couldn't. He knew victory when he saw it, and this was it.

She waited there by the bed, shaken to the core, and tried not to think of what she might be feeling come morning.

Tucker casually threw back the covers, and she braced herself for his touch, but he walked past her, instead.

She heard the click of the bedroom door's lock, then couldn't avoid looking at him when he came to stand directly in front of her.

The lights were off in the room, but the moon was out tonight and it was shining in through the window. It caught the golden highlights in his hair and touched on the ripples and hollows on his chest.

She closed her eyes and tried to calm herself, but couldn't manage that at this moment.

"Come to me, Rebecca." He held out his arms. "Take that one step, just one, and I'll do the rest. I need to know that this is as much your decision as mine."

She hesitated in taking that first step into the abyss, the one that would put her firmly within his grasp, within his power.

But then, she'd always been there. She'd never managed to escape. Maybe she never would.

What was it about him?

What?

Would she ever understand it? Would she be able to survive it this time?

"Just a step," he coaxed.

She stood up. The blood rushed to her head, and the heat flamed in her cheeks. There was no turning back now. There was nowhere to run that he wouldn't find her.

"Come on, Rebecca. You can do it."

He was smiling, teasing her now that he knew he'd won.

He was her downfall, her siren's song.

Rebecca felt a little too unsteady on her feet to manage the step that seemed so important to him. He'd have to settle for a hand, instead.

She took a deep breath, hoping it would steady her, and reached out to touch those subtle curves of muscles in his upper arm.

He was hot to the touch, scorching hot. She was surprised she didn't see the steam rising off of him.

Rebecca lost her nerve and went to pull away from him, but he caught her first and pressed her hand back to his arm.

"Don't stop," he said, and something in his voice gave her the courage to continue.

She let her hand glide up his arm to his shoulder, then down to those little blond curls on his chest.

He groaned and closed his eyes. A fine sheen of moisture covered his chest, and her heart beat even faster than before.

He was trembling, yet utterly still.

And she was lost.

The power vibrated around them, closing in on them like a force field, binding them together and locking out the world around them.

She touched him, fingertips furrowing through those curls, up the center of his chest, past the pulse point under his chin, brushing past his lips and then along his clenched jaw.

She shivered and swayed toward him. He was swaying on his feet, as well.

She took both hands, palms flat against his chest, and made little circles with her thumbs.

"Mmmm." He made a long, low sound of pure pleasure.

He brought his hand up to cup her jaw, to caress her cheek, then slip into her hair. He pulled out the pins, one by one, until her hair fell to just beyond her shoulder.

He took a handful of it and buried his nose in it, inhaling deeply, then pulling it back so that he could tease her ear with his mouth.

"Touch me," he whispered.

Rebecca blushed, knowing what he wanted. Her hands made their way down to his belly, then lower. She remembered—yes, she thought as she found him fully aroused—she remembered exactly how he felt.

He gasped, then groaned, shivered with pleasure, while she teased and stroked him.

"Oh, Rebecca!"

She smiled for the first time since she came into the room, because the power wasn't all his.

It was hers, too. And it was such a heady feeling. Such pleasure came from knowing that the things he did to her, she could do to him, as well.

It told her that she wasn't the only one taking a risk here tonight.

"Rebecca?"

"Hmmm?" His skin was silky-soft there, satin on steel.

"If you keep that up, I'm going to make a hell of a mess."

Laughter bubbled up inside her and spilled out. She was soaring, so free, so high above all the worries that had been holding her down just a few minutes ago.

Inside her, the passion danced and sizzled, like a drop of water on a hot grill.

And she heard the music, felt the rhythm and the throb—the desire she'd thought she'd lost—spiral up inside her, setting her free. She felt so free.

"Rebecca?" he said in warning, because she hadn't stopped touching him. She couldn't.

"Come to bed with me." She invited him this time.

He came willingly.

They fell together on the bed in a tangle of arms and legs and clothes.

And it was just the same.

Inside, she felt just the way she remembered. He felt just the way she remembered.

His hands, his lips, the muscles in his arms, the brush of his thighs against hers. The heat, the need, the passion, as overwhelming as it always had been.

She couldn't breathe, couldn't wait, couldn't bear for it to end, because she wasn't ready to let go of this feeling. How could she ever let go of this?

Her clothes were gone, most of them, anyway, and his mouth settled over her breast.

His body settled over hers and he was pushing inside her, inch by inch, slowly, powerfully, into the heat of her.

And she was lost.

She woke deep in the night, naked in her tangled sheets and her warm bed with a man's arms around her, her body pressed against the length of his.

She'd fallen asleep in his arms.

Rebecca went to move away from him. She needed to think, and she couldn't do that when he was so close.

But he wouldn't let go. She thought he was asleep, but he wasn't, and he wouldn't let go.

"Stay," he said softly, his lips against the top of her head. "Just for... another minute or two."

There was a catch in his voice, a hint of something she didn't recognize. If he had been anyone else, she would have said a vulnerability.

But she was the vulnerable one, the one in danger of losing herself in him all over again.

"Tucker?"

His arms tightened around her again. They held her still when she would have turned around to face him. But her curiosity wouldn't let it go at that. She tried again, and this time he let her go.

Her first instinct was to get up off the bed, to put some distance between herself and him, but something else— that unfamiliar tone to his voice—kept her there.

She eased out of his arms and rolled over. He was lying on his side, facing her. He was staring at her so intently, looking for something, searching inside her soul.

For what?

What more did he want from her?

What did she have left to give?

He took her chin in his hand, ran his thumb along her jaw, then kissed her softly on the lips. And once again, her body set out to betray her.

"I've missed you, Rebecca," he said, his voice low and rough with emotion.

She swallowed hard, not sure how to respond, not sure that she even had to. She'd already shown him how very much she missed him. Did she have to say it, as well?

She stared at him through the darkness, watched as he came closer and closer to kiss her again, lingering this time, pressing closer in a hot, shimmering touch that made her think of ashes smoldering in a fireplace.

It was so easy to bring up the fire again.

Rebecca shivered in the midst of the heat. Then, when he would have pulled away, she put her hand on the side of his face to hold him to her.

What was she going to do with him? What was he going to do to her?

He kissed her again. She heard the rustle of the sheets as he pushed them out of the way and pressed his body to hers.

Her hand caressed his cheek and— Puzzled, she broke off the kiss. She couldn't believe it.

There were tears on his cheek.

"Tucker?"

"I love you, Rebecca," he said, using that same rough, emotion-packed tone.

She was speechless. He'd told her that before, and she'd tried not to dwell on it, tried not even to remember it, because she just didn't know what to make of it.

She didn't know how to deal with it, and it frightened her too much to even contemplate—loving him again— having him love her.

"I don't..." That was simply all she could manage, because she didn't know what to say and because he had turned his head so that he could press a kiss into her palm.

"Rebecca, do you think if I say it enough, someday you might believe it?"

She stared at him. "I don't know. I don't understand."

She put her hand on his other cheek and found a tear there, as well. She followed its path with one finger, still having a hard time accepting what she'd found.

He was a man who rarely showed his emotions, a man who'd rather tell a joke and make her laugh than talk about anything that might be bothering him. And she'd never seen him like this.

He kissed her again, fiercely. His arms came around her and gathered her close as they lay side by side on the bed.

Her breasts nestled against his chest, his arousal pressed against her belly and his legs intertwined with hers.

"Give me a chance," he said between his long, drugging kisses. "Give me a chance to make you believe it."

She shivered with pleasure and held on to him tight, held on to the moment, held on to the night.

If only they could hold on to the night and never deal with the realities of their mixed-up lives, with the insecurities and fears and past wrongs that could never be made right.

Rebecca gave herself up to his touch and his fire. He rolled over onto his back and took her with him, settled her on top of him and with his hands on her hips, urged her into a long, slow, sensuous rhythm as old as time.

They made love one more time before the dawn betrayed them.

Rebecca lay there on her back and watched the light sneak in through the blinds. She was exhausted and exhilarated, more confused than she'd ever been in her life, and she was scared. She was so very scared.

In the night, she'd told him with her body what she'd refused to put into words—she'd given him another chance.

"Mmmm," Tucker murmured and buried his nose in the curve of her neck.

He was lying on top of her, just a little to the right, just enough so she could breathe, and she was running her hands in long, slow strokes over the muscles in his back and his buttocks.

Yes, she thought as she watched the sunshine grow brighter. She'd told him all he needed to know last night. She was far from indifferent to him. And God help her now that he knew.

Rebecca felt goose bumps rising on her flesh as he nipped at her neck with his teeth and knew she had to stop him right now or she'd never get him out of here.

"Tucker?"

"Hmmm?"

"Sammy's going to be getting up soon. You've got to get out of here," she said, uncomfortable with him beside her in her bed in the harsh light of day.

He waited and watched, just long enough to worry her, then rolled off of her, put his underwear and his pants back on, then sat on the side of the bed facing her.

"Okay, I'll get out of here, in a minute. But first, you and I have some talking to do."

"About what?" she dared to ask, ever so innocently.

"The price of tea in China?" He said it lightly, but she recognized it for the warning that it was. She wasn't going to get away from him until they'd settled some things.

Rebecca tucked the sheet around her and sat up, leaning against a pillow propped against the headboard and staring down at her hand so she didn't have to look at him.

She'd expected regrets come morning, and she was sure they were inside her head somewhere. But for right now, she was simply exhausted and her brain had turned to mush.

She felt curiously numb, as if the sensations and emotions were simply too much for her to take in and her overloaded brain had just shut down.

He took her hands in his and ran his thumbs over hers, back and forth over her ring finger. Her hands were bare, save for the small gold band, her grandmother's, that she wore on the third finger of her right hand.

He twisted it back and forth on her finger, then turned his attention to her left hand, to the telltale white strip of skin on the otherwise tanned hand that told him until recently, there'd been a ring there.

Her engagement ring from Brian.

It seemed like a million years ago that she'd been planning, then postponing, then planning again, to marry Brian.

Tucker stared down at that white band of skin.

"When I decided I had to come find Sammy, I was certain you and Brian were married," he said. "And I never even imagined that the two of us..."

He paused, clasped his fingers with hers and gave her a weak smile. "I think I'm getting ahead of myself. When I found out you weren't married, everything changed. I thought Sammy'd had a father all this time. I didn't think I'd ever have a chance to really be his father, and that it would be selfish of me to even try because Brian had already taken over that role.

"I thought you had a husband, Rebecca. I thought you loved him and you were happy and... I just never thought there'd be another chance for us, even though it didn't take long for me to realize that was what I wanted.

"And even when I knew you were free, for the longest time I thought it was hopeless.

"But it's not. I mean—it must not be hopeless. Not after last night."

"Tucker?" She shook her head back and forth. "It was just sex. It was good, but—"

"Don't even try to tell me it didn't mean anything to you." She'd made him angry. "I know you better than that, Rebecca."

She thought about arguing, but was afraid of the methods he'd use to convince her she was wrong. So she held her tongue and let him continue.

"I love Sammy, and Sammy loves me. I need him, Rebecca, and you know he needs me, too. He wants us to be a family again, and so do I."

A family?

"We are his family, Tucker. His mother and his father. We'll always be tied together because of Sammy."

He stared at her for the longest time, then shook his head and laughed, sadly.

"Do you really not know? Did you think I just wanted to get you into bed with me again? Did you think this was about my ego or something?"

"I . . ." She was afraid to even answer him, afraid to have him answer her. "I just don't know."

He cursed and got to his feet, the tension pushing him to move, anywhere. He raked his hand back through his hair, then stopped by the window to lean against the casing and stare out at the coming day.

"I know you're not ready for this, Rebecca, and I've tried to wait, but you know patience has never been one of my better qualities." He walked back to the bed.

She felt it give beneath his weight as he sat down beside her, facing her, waiting for her to look at him.

"Rebecca?"

Her eyes came up to meet his, and she had this desperate urge to flee from that incredibly intense look in his eyes. He'd already turned her world upside down. What more could he possibly do?

What, indeed?

"I guess I must be doing something wrong if you have no idea. You don't, do you?"

She shook her head in wonder.

He tilted his head to the right and moved in slowly, settling his lips over hers in a slow, sweet, unnerving kiss.

"I want you to be my wife again."

Chapter 15

She sat there—naked save for the sheet she clutched to her breasts—in the bed where he'd proven to her, beyond the shadow of a doubt, that she still had feelings for him.

Denying it would do her no good.

But marriage?

Marriage?

Something had warned her, before he spoke, to brace herself, to prepare for something. But she'd never dreamed—not this. She never would have believed he could want to be married to her again.

And, yes, she had entertained thoughts that his whole pursuit of her had a lot to do with his ego, maybe a little curiosity, a little bit of for-old-times'-sake thrown in.

But she'd never imagined this.

She'd believed that he would turn her life upside down—he already had—but she'd also been sure that the day would come when things would get back to normal again, when he would be gone and she would be picking up the pieces of her life.

Again.

If she could this time.

But marriage?

"Tucker, I'd never interfere with your relationship with Sammy, if that's what you're worried about. And we don't have to be married to be a family for him."

"I know."

"And Sammy understands that. I know he's upset right now, but he—"

"It's not about Sammy," he said, watching her every move. "It's about us."

"Tucker..." She shook her head in wonder.

"I love you, Rebecca. I'm not sure if I even knew what the words meant the first time I said them to you, all those years ago, but I do now. I know so much more now than I did then."

He went still. His jaw was rigid and his eyes were so bright, so intense.

"You still feel something for me. I know you do. I can feel it every time I touch you."

His trump card. She knew he was going to get around to that sooner or later. And there was nothing she could say to it.

She felt it every time he touched her, and she couldn't hide it from him.

"I'm not the man I used to be, Rebecca."

"I know that."

He smiled like a man who knew he was gaining ground with her all the time.

"I won't hurt you this time, Rebecca. I'll cherish you. I'll be thankful for every day we have together."

She wanted to plead with him to stop. She wanted to run from him, or turn back the clock, to go back to the time when she hadn't heard from him in years.

"Oh, Tucker."

"I've been lonely, Rebecca. Empty. You've felt it, too. You told me so."

She closed her eyes. She remembered the loneliness, remembered the day she'd faced the idea of spending the rest of her life alone, just her and Sammy. The day she'd said goodbye to the idea of having more children and having the kind of family she'd dreamed of when she was a little girl.

It wasn't going to happen. It didn't when she was married to Tucker and not in all those years of trying to build a life with Brian.

But to try again with Tucker?

God, it scared her to death just thinking about it.

"I— Oh, Tucker. I couldn't make it through losing you again. I just couldn't do it."

Rebecca wished she could pull the words back inside her, but she couldn't. She'd given him a powerful weapon over her—her greatest fear—that she'd fall in love with him all over again and then lose him.

It frightened her just to want to be with him again, because she knew this time it would kill her to lose him.

Rebecca waited, holding her breath, to see what he could possibly do next.

He fished around in the pocket of his jeans, and she wondered why did it have to be him who made her feel this way? Why?

A flash of light brought her head up, and she saw something in his hand. No, on his finger.

A ring, perched on the tip of his thumb, catching the light shining in the window, leaving her absolutely speechless, absolutely paralyzed with fear.

She opened her mouth, struggling with the words.

"No," he said, hushing her with a finger against her lips. "Don't say anything. I know you don't love me anymore, but you feel something for me. And maybe in time you could come to love me again."

Which was exactly what scared her to death.

She watched in shock as Tucker took advantage of the element of surprise. It shouldn't have surprised her, because Tucker made full use of any advantage he'd ever had. He slipped that big diamond on her finger, covering up the white band of skin, and held it there when her impulse was to tear it off as fast as she could.

"Try it out, Rebecca. Give it a chance." He kissed her hand, the palm, and she felt the touch jet through her entire body. "We'll make it work this time."

And then he scooped his shirt up off the floor and left.

She couldn't believe he just left, right then in the middle of this.

Left her with his ring on her finger.

She jerked it off, hurting her finger in the process. Then she sat there, naked in her bed, staring at the ring he'd left behind.

"Rebecca?" her mother said.

"Mmmm?" Rebecca quit fidgeting with her tea bag and set it aside.

"Do you want to tell me what's wrong? Or do I have to guess?"

Rebecca heaped sugar into her tea. She was sleepy and still in shock over what had happened the night before. And, as for explaining it to her mother, she couldn't even begin to understand all that had happened in the course of only one night, so how could she hope to explain it to anyone else.

"Well," her mother said, "if I had to guess, I'd say it's Tucker."

"Good guess," Rebecca said as she stirred her tea and took a sip.

She felt like laughing at what she was about to say, except there was nothing funny about it. And she had this sinking feeling that if she started laughing, she might never be able to stop.

Rebecca had a vision of herself laughing hysterically, while big, strong men in the starched white coats came to pick her up and take her to her very own padded cell, where she could laugh away the rest of her days in peace.

"I think," she said, fighting the hysteria, "that Tucker thinks we're engaged."

Her mother didn't get ruffled, not ever. Hurricanes, tornadoes, fires, floods—Rebecca would bet that her mother could come through them all without so much as breaking a nail or messing up her hair. Not that her mother was cold or unfeeling or any of those things. She wasn't. She just put an inordinate amount of importance on her ability to maintain her composure.

It held—even now—and Rebecca once again wished she could be just a little bit more like her mother.

Composure was a quality she valued greatly at the moment.

"Mother?" she said when she could stand it no more. "Say something."

Her mother, incredibly composed, paused to ponder her question. "You're afraid he thinks you're engaged?"

Rebecca nodded.

"And I'm just wondering, dear.... It seems like that would have to be a mutual decision—an engagement."

"Not where Tucker's concerned."

Rebecca couldn't help it anymore. She started to laugh, a sound that frightened her.

She was living on the edge, and she wanted to get off.

Her mother laid a hand on Rebecca's arm—no doubt hoping to be a steadying influence.

"That may be true," Margaret said. "Then I'd have to wonder if you gave him any reason to believe that the two of you might be engaged."

Pictures of the night they'd spent together flashed by in front of her closed eyes. The sounds, the scent, the heat.

Rebecca heard his fierce declaration of love, his tender promise that he would never hurt her again, his plea for another chance.

And she could still see the ring—its light brilliant as it glittered in the morning sunshine coming in her bedroom window.

"I never said I'd marry him," she protested, then dangerously near her breaking point, laughed again. It sounded so ridiculous, even to her. But there it was. That was what happened. "He just left before I had a chance to tell him that I wouldn't."

"Rebecca—"

"I know," she cried. "It's crazy—I'm crazy! He makes me crazy."

She looked up at her mother. Rebecca hadn't come running to her mother with her troubles in all the time she'd been on her own since her marriage to Tucker had fallen apart, yet here she was, feeling like she was twelve and the world was crashing down around her. This was what he'd done to her.

"What am I going to do, Mom?"

Her mother smiled, so serenely. "Well, Tucker wants to marry you again."

Rebecca nodded.

"And Sammy?"

"Has come to love his father very much."

As she made her way to the bar at the corner of the family room, picked up one bottle, discarded it and started searching among the remaining ones, her mother said, "I don't think sherry will do. Do you, dear?"

Rebecca laughed for real this time. "No," she said through her smile.

Her mother was incredible, Rebecca thought as she watched her pour two generous servings of some dark, amber-colored liquid.

Rebecca gulped hers, hoping it would help to calm her, but doubting that anything short of unconsciousness would be able to do that.

As she sipped her drink, Margaret said, "Tucker doesn't give up. If he intends to be a real father to Sammy, which I believe he does, and he wants to marry you again, he won't give up—not ever. He doesn't know how to quit when there's something he wants."

Rebecca dropped her head into her trembling hands for a moment, then clasped her fingers together in front of her face.

She'd already concluded the exact same thing. It was the reason her panic was so great. He wouldn't give up. He wouldn't go away.

And eventually, she would betray herself.

Because despite all that had happened and all the many ways they'd hurt each other—she still wanted him in two very important ways.

She wanted him for Sammy, for the family that they could be, the one they should have been all along.

And she wanted him for herself, for that mysterious, hidden, feminine side of her that she'd thought had died—the one he'd so miraculously revived. That part of her wanted him desperately.

It was just her heart and her brain that were holding out. Just those two little parts that remembered all too vividly what he'd done to her before.

So there she was, at war with herself and unable to see any resolution to it—trapped as neatly as she'd been nine years ago when faced with a gorgeous, determined, sinfully sexy man who'd decided he couldn't live without her—at least not at the moment.

"Mother, do you think a person can change that much?"

The hand was back on her arm, holding on tight, giving a squeeze of reassurance.

"I think that it takes some people much longer than others to figure out what's truly important to them. But it doesn't matter what I think, Rebecca. What do you think? Do you believe that a person can change that much?"

Rebecca looked up at the sky through the terrace window. "I just don't know."

Rebecca had another drink with her mother, then set out to find her father.

She left the family room, crossed through the kitchen, formal living room and dining room, then down the hallway to her father's study.

She'd decided she'd rather tell him herself about what was going on than to let him hear about it from Tucker—and get Tucker's version of events.

She was almost to the door, getting ready to knock, when she heard her father's voice.

"Have you reasons to be hopeful?"

"A few," Tucker answered.

Damn, she thought. She was too late.

"Maybe this will get you back into the family in each and every way. Why don't you come back to the firm, as well?"

Rebecca went still as old, familiar insecurities came flooding back. The firm. The money. The power. All her father's with no one to leave it to except a daughter who simply wasn't interested.

But lots of people were interested.

Lots of men.

And some of them had one particular shortcut in mind when they thought of becoming her father's heir apparent to Tallahassee's most influential law firm—some of them planned to cut a path right through her heart.

She'd always wondered if Tucker had been one of those men.

Her father said something about her and Tucker getting back together again—pressed for more details and offered to help in any way that he could. Tucker laughed and said something she missed.

Back to the firm again, the bait her father had.

And then she went cold all over.

"I don't know," Tucker said. "Same deal as before?"

"If that's what it takes," her father said.

Tucker laughed again. "It would almost be worth it. Almost."

Deal? Rebecca thought as the numbness rolled over her.

They had a deal before. And they were working on one now.

She turned to go, trying not to run because she didn't want anyone to hear her, because she couldn't face him right now.

A deal.

Her and the firm. The firm and her.

"Ouch!" She yelped as her foot caught the corner of a dainty table in the hallway, banging her toe and knocking a vase to the floor.

It crashed as it hit the hardwood flooring, and she heard voices calling out from the study.

"Rebecca?" Tucker called as he rounded the corner and saw her hurrying out the patio door.

Remembering what he'd been saying to her father only moments ago—what she'd obviously overheard—he cursed and ran after her.

Tucker caught up with her in the garden and knew by the look on her face that he had an uphill battle ahead of him if he was ever going to make her understand. He held her by the arm to keep her from getting away from him, and she glared at him beyond a mask of hurt and anger.

"Rebecca? I don't know what you heard, but—"

"I heard everything! I just wish I'd heard it years ago, maybe the first time you asked me to marry you."

She tried to pull away from him, but he held her easily. He wasn't about to let go.

Rebecca jerked her arm back again and glared at him. "I didn't know how badly you wanted that law firm, but you must want it dearly to marry me for it again."

Tucker was furious, more so than he'd been in years. "I have a job—one that I happen to like very much. I don't want the damned firm, but if I did, I wouldn't have to marry you to get it."

She glared at him for at least thirty seconds, then roared back. "I heard you in there just now, making a deal. Same one as before, you said. It would almost be worth it, you said. I heard it all, so don't you dare deny it."

"You don't even know what you heard," he said, not even trying to disguise his anger.

He'd been so hopeful this morning when he'd left her. Left his ring on her finger. Left her body still warm from his touch. Left with the taste of her lips on his.

"Think about it, Rebecca. If I'd wanted the firm, I could have had it by now. I was still there after we divorced—and your father wanted me to run the place until I could turn it over to Sammy."

"I heard you," she insisted. "Talking about marrying me again and coming back to work there and a deal—the same one as before. I heard you say it."

"Fine," he said, turning toward the house and pulling her along with him. "You want to know about our deal, you can hear it from your father. Maybe you'll believe him, because it's obvious you're not going to believe a damned thing I say."

Rebecca didn't say a word as they made their way inside, down the hall, past the broken vase and into her father's study.

"Rebecca?" her father said. "Are you all right?"

"Tell her about our deal." Tucker nearly roared with it.

Samuel Harwell looked from one of them to the other, then back again.

"Tell her," Tucker insisted.

"Well, there's not much to tell," he said to Rebecca. "I wanted Tucker to come to work for me. He wanted to marry you. And I guess, sometimes, I tend to get a little too involved in other people's business."

The understatement of the year, Tucker thought.

Rebecca couldn't argue with that.

"So," her father continued, "we made a deal. Tucker said he'd come to work for me if I kept my nose out of his relationship with you."

Rebecca's eyes flew from her father's to Tucker's, and he watched as the color flooded her pale cheeks.

"That's it?" she said in disbelief.

"That's it," Tucker told her, then turned to Sam. "Would you mind if we used your study for a few minutes?"

"Of course not."

Tucker walked very slowly to the door and closed it behind Rebecca's father. Then he stood there, facing the door, afraid of the damage this whole thing had done to the already fragile bond between them.

Tucker cursed under his breath. He made a fist and thought about how much satisfaction he could get out of trying to put it through the door. He cursed some more, instead.

"Why did you marry me, Tucker?"

He gathered his courage and turned at the soft-spoken question. "I thought it was obvious, but I— Did you really think all I wanted was your father's law practice?"

"Sometimes," she admitted without looking at him. She was gazing out the window. "I know that when we met, marriage wasn't something you were particularly interested in."

"No, I wasn't," he said, forcing himself to be honest with her, hating himself when he saw her draw her arms around her middle and hold on tight. "But I hardly knew you then. I didn't know ... I didn't know how powerful this thing between us would be. I didn't know that I just wouldn't be able to walk away from you. That I wouldn't be able to forget you."

Tucker searched his mind for the memories of that crazy time after they'd first met, but it was difficult. The feelings had been so powerful, so overwhelming, until there'd been nothing but Rebecca and his need for her.

It had blinded him to his memories of his own parents' terrible marriage, to his own vows never to risk such a thing as marriage.

It had blinded him to everything but her.

"Rebecca, I needed you more than I needed my next breath."

"You wanted to go to bed with me," she said, finally turning to face him.

"I wanted to go everywhere with you. I thought you knew that."

But he could see the doubts in her eyes, the self-doubts that he probably should have seen a long time ago.

He walked to where she stood by the window and let himself touch her hair.

He gathered one curl between his fingers and remembered how it had smelled last night when his nose had been buried against her neck. He remembered how it felt to have her above him, kissing him, with her hair trailing after her, brushing across his chest and his stomach.

He wanted that again. He wanted that forever. He would make it last, this time, forever. If she gave him the chance.

"Rebecca?"

He reached for her again, but she sidestepped and got out of reach.

"I have to go," she said with a tremor in her voice. "Sammy's going to be home from school soon."

"All right." He shoved his hands into his pockets to keep himself from touching her again, from grabbing onto her when he might not be able to let go, not ever. "But we have a lot of other things we need to talk about."

"I know," she said. "But not now. I just can't handle it right now."

And as he watched her go, he wondered if she ever would be able to handle the things in their past.

Chapter 16

Rebecca hurried down the hall toward the Coastal Commission's meeting room and hoped she wasn't too late to get a seat.

The group was hearing an appeal today from the paper mill company over whether the permits obtained years ago were still valid or whether the company must obtain new ones.

It was a big meeting. If Rebecca's citizen's group lost today and the paper mill company was able to use its old permits, Rebecca might as well give up.

She was nervous—as much about the outcome of the hearing as she was about how Tucker would handle it. Her friends at the various environmental groups were raving about him. He was a tiger, a real fighter, they said.

She wanted to believe them.

She wanted to believe a lot of things these days.

A part of her wanted to turn her back on everything

that had happened in the past—to simply put it behind her. Maybe that's where it belonged.

A part of her wanted to put his ring on her finger and believe that he'd changed as much as he said he had.

And the other part of her was just scared.

She turned the corner, caught sight of Tucker's sandy-blond head in the corner of the room and wondered if she could make her way over to talk with him.

She was worried about Sammy and wanted to talk to him about it. Jimmy Horton practically lived at their house these days since his mother was so upset and his father was still retrieving possessions to take from their house to his new house.

And the strain on Jimmy was taking its toll on Sammy.

He was moody and withdrawn, frightened for sure, underneath it all, but Rebecca hadn't been able to get past his mood.

Tucker looked up then, and she was about to make her way over to him, but he motioned her the other way, toward his office down the hall. It would be better to talk there, she decided.

She was at Tucker's office door when she nearly bumped into Brian.

"Hi," she said, surprised and a little uneasy. She still felt guilty over everything that had happened between them. "What are you doing here?"

"I came to town to sign the closing papers on the house and watch over the movers, but then my mother came to see me. She told me— I can't believe what she told me."

Rebecca could just imagine what his mother had heard from her mother. They still lived next door to each other, and they were still the best of friends.

"Brian—"

He grabbed her left hand and stared at her bare ring finger.

"Tell me it's not true, Rebecca. Tell me," he demanded.

"What did your mother say?"

"That you were going to marry Tucker again. I told her she was crazy, but now I'm starting to wonder if I'm not the one who's crazy."

"You?" Rebecca said, playing for time.

"Yeah, me. I've been waiting for you to come to your senses and come back to me."

"Oh, Brian." Rebecca felt absolutely sick.

And then she felt an arm slide around her waist from behind, felt it ease her back against a familiar male body.

"I wouldn't hold my breath if I were you," Tucker said, his light tone in complete contrast to the tension she felt in his rock-hard body.

Brian ignored him and kept his eyes on Rebecca—though he was clearly furious at the way Tucker was touching her, at what the familiarity of Tucker's touch must be saying to him.

"Rebecca, tell me you're not going to marry this lying cheat—"

"You want to talk about lies?" Tucker cut in. "I bet there're a lot of things you haven't been honest about with Rebecca over the past few years."

Tucker was furious. He stepped away from Rebecca and got right up to Brian's face. "And you sure as hell owe me a lot of answers," he said.

Rebecca didn't know what he was talking about, but Brian did. He went stock still and silent, seething in his tracks.

"What in the world is going on between the two of you?" she said.

Her question silenced them both. They stared at each other, each daring the other to explain.

Rebecca felt a nasty chill work its way up her spine.

They were keeping something from her.

"Excuse me?" said a young man as he hesitantly stepped into the fray. "Mr. Malloy, the chairman's ready to begin now, and we need you."

Tucker looked like he was ready to hit someone, and she prayed he wouldn't. He glared at Brian and clenched his fist.

Rebecca laid her hand on his arm, the muscle tight with tension.

"We'll be right there, Andy," Tucker said, putting his hand on top of Rebecca's as he turned to face her. "I told you three days ago that we had some other things to talk about it. Well, this is it, but it's going to have to wait a little while longer. I've got to get into this meeting."

"Okay," she said, still feeling the chill.

Tucker turned and left.

Rebecca watched him go, then turned back to Brian. She was torn—didn't know which way to turn. She wanted to know what they were talking about, yet she didn't. She wanted to talk to Brian, to try to make some peace with him, yet she didn't see how they could.

"I... I need to get in there. It's the paper mill appeal and..."

"I'll go with you," he said.

Rebecca steeled herself for more trouble and walked into the meeting room beside him. They managed to find two seats together near the back of the room just as the chairman rapped twice with the gavel to start the meeting.

Brian had his arm resting on the back of Rebecca's seat, and his touch made her almost as uncomfortable as the look in Tucker's eyes as he stared at Brian from across the room.

"Tell me you're not going back to him, Rebecca," Brian whispered, too close to her left ear.

She looked up, caught Tucker's eye and felt absolutely torn.

How could a woman want something so badly and be so frightened of it at the same time?

"I don't know what I'm going to do," she told Brian.

"Are you insane, Rebecca? You can't trust the man—"

"Wait a minute," she said. "What's going on up front?"

A few of the commission members looked quite annoyed. Tucker stood before the chairman answering his questions.

"We all came here to hear this appeal today," Jim Gardner told Tucker.

"I'm sorry, Mr. Chairman. We're just not prepared to proceed today. We've just been given some new information that has a direct bearing on the case, and we haven't had time to check into it."

Rebecca had Brian on one side and David Wilkins from the Sierra Club on the other. "What the hell is he doing?" they both asked her.

"I don't know," she said.

The commissioners called upon Tucker to explain himself some more, but they didn't get a lot out of him.

And the more Rebecca heard, the worse she felt. What in the world was he doing? She'd talked to him last night about the hearing, and he'd told her he felt good about his chances of winning before the commission.

Of course, the paper mill company would appeal, but that would take months, probably years, and anything could happen in a year or so.

So what was he doing now?

"I told you that you can't trust him," Brian said.

And she didn't say anything to that. She couldn't, because she worried about that very thing herself.

"He's going to roll over on this permit, isn't he?" Brian continued.

"No, he's not," she insisted, wishing she had no doubts herself.

The chairman's gavel fell, adjourning the meeting for thirty minutes or so while they waited for the parties to the next appeal to arrive.

Half a dozen more people came up to Rebecca to ask her what Tucker was doing, but she couldn't help them.

Tucker brushed his way past a couple of reporters—as closemouthed with them as he had been in front of the commission—then made his way over to Rebecca.

"Let's talk in my office," he said, taking her by the elbow and propelling her through the crowd. "You coming?" he said over his shoulder to Brian.

"No," Brian quickly replied.

Tucker marched down the hall with Rebecca to his office, closed the door behind them and pointed her toward the love seat, then he pulled a chair up so that he sat directly in front of her.

She had trouble meeting his eyes. She looked everywhere except at him, until there was nowhere else to look.

He looked awful, and she dreaded even more what was coming.

"God, just tell me," she said finally.

He was leaning forward, his elbows resting on his knees, his head bent down looking at his hands. Then he took her hands in his and held them there between them

"We have to talk about Cheryl Atkinson."

"No, we don't," Rebecca said, desperate to avoid the subject all together.

"Rebecca." He held on to her hands and wouldn't let go. "She may walk into that meeting room in about fifteen minutes. She's taking over for one of the companies fighting us on the wetlands appeal that's up next."

Tucker winced at the look in her eyes, the one he remembered. She'd looked just like this the day she walked into his office and found him in Cheryl's arms.

And in that instant, as he watched her eyes, he'd had this awful, sinking feeling that he'd made a terrible mistake, one he couldn't take back and couldn't make up for no matter what he did.

It had all seemed so simple at the time and so stupid now, so cowardly.

How could he make her understand?

"Rebecca—"

She jerked her hands out of his.

"Have you been seeing her, too?"

"No." He exploded with it, then regretted it instantly

"But you came here knowing she was still here, that you'd be working with her."

"I didn't even know she was in town until she took over this wetlands case last week. And it didn't even occur to me to ask if she was still in town, because she was the furthest thing from my mind when I came back here All I was thinking about was you. You and Sammy."

"But you didn't always feel that way, did you?"

Rebecca had slid over to the corner of the love seat, as far away from him as she could get, and she was shaking.

Tucker wanted to go to her, wanted to take her in his arms, but he didn't think she'd let him touch her. He stood up and walked to the window, shoved his hands into his pockets and looked out at the dreary, rain-soaked day.

It was November. Christmas would be here soon, and he'd hoped that they would all spend this Christmas together, their first ever.

And right now, he felt it all slipping through his fingers.

"That's what we need to talk about, Rebecca. It was a setup. I knew you were coming to the office that day, and I set you up to find us together."

He turned away from the window so that he could see her face. She didn't believe him. Hell, there were times when he had trouble believing himself what he'd done.

"How can you expect me to believe that?" she said. "Why would you want me to find you with another woman?"

"Because of Brian. He said he still loved you. He wanted to marry you. And he was willing to be a father to Sammy." Tucker struggled with the admission, even now, after all this time. "He was going to be everything I couldn't be, to give you and Sammy all the things I couldn't give you."

"What?" she said, and he doubted she'd believed a word that came out of his mouth.

"I told you, Rebecca. I heard the two of you in the garden at your parents' house, that day he came back to town. You couldn't tell him that you didn't love him anymore, and you sure as hell weren't happy with me."

She shook her head back and forth. "What are you getting at, Tucker?"

"I heard Brian was thinking of leaving town, and I didn't see any way that you and I were going to make our marriage work."

"Go on," she said hesitantly.

"We had a child to think about, and I kept seeing my-self, my parents and the bitterness and anger and uncer-tainty." He paused, trying to make some sense out of his jumbled thoughts, knowing that he wasn't explaining himself well, if there was a way to explain it well.

"Rebecca, I'm not proud of what I did, and I'm not trying to say it was the right thing to do or that I did it all for you and Sammy. If I could take it back—if any of us could ever change anything that we'd done...

"I made a deal with Brian."

There, he'd finally said it. And he wasn't sure if it would help or if it would hurt, but it was the truth. He'd promised himself that he would be honest with her, no matter how much it hurt.

"You did what?" Rebecca turned absolutely white.

Tucker swallowed hard and made himself continue. "I knew there was no way our marriage would survive. I knew Brian loved you. So I made a deal with him."

"I told him that I would get out of your life, yours and Sammy's, totally, if he still wanted to marry you and if he promised to love Sammy like he would his own son."

Rebecca laughed, an out-of-control sound that held no pleasure. "I...I can't believe this."

"Ask Brian. He'll tell you. Or your mother. If she hasn't known all along, she's at least suspected."

"No," she said. "I didn't mean that I think you're ly-ing about it now. I mean—I just can't believe this. Ar you telling me that you weren't having an affair with Cheryl Atkinson?''

"I never touched her until that day at the office. I swear it. She was just there, Rebecca. She was available and more than willing.''

Rebecca stared down at her hands, clenched in her lap. "And Brian went along with this?''

"He didn't know what I was going to do. Hell, I didn't know myself until Cheryl showed up at my office that day, and I knew you'd be coming by to see your father and that you'd probably poke your head in my door to say hello. I knew if you saw us together, if I let you think . . . I knew that would be the end of it for you and that Brian would be there to pick up the pieces.''

"And Brian went along with it?''

"I think he would have done anything to get you back.''

Just as Tucker would do anything right now to get her to come back to him.

And now he wondered if he'd waited too late to tell her this. He would have done it before, except he didn't think she would believe him. He didn't think it would matter to her, but lately he felt like he had a chance to get her back.

He'd been trying to figure out how to tell her, and he'd been hoping that he could put it off just a little while longer to give her some time to learn to trust him again.

But now it had all blown up in his face.

"Rebecca, I'm not trying to make this out to be some noble thing I did. I honestly wanted you and Sammy to be happy, and I thought you would be with Brian. But at the same time, I was a coward, and this looked like the easy way out, a way to ease my conscience just a little for making such a damned mess of our lives.''

"Do you think that you—"

Someone knocked on the closed door, and Tucker wanted to scream in frustration. He needed more time. He had a lot of other things he wanted to say to her, and if he quit now, he was afraid he might never get that chance.

"Mr. Malloy?" The knock sounded again.

Reluctantly, Tucker went to the door and opened it. "Yes, Andy?"

"The chairman's ready to hear the wetlands appeal."

"Okay, I'll be right there." Tucker turned back to Rebecca, watched her as she sat there white-faced and refused to meet his eyes. "Rebecca, this won't take long. Please don't leave."

She peeked at him, then looked away without saying a word. No promises there.

Tucker took a deep breath and walked down the hall. He met Brian halfway and wondered if he would lose his job if he decked the man in the hallway.

Probably.

And Rebecca would probably be mad as hell about it.

Plus half the town would be talking about it come morning.

"Damn you," Tucker said as he shouldered his way past the man.

And he damned himself while he was at it.

Rebecca sat there in Tucker's office, wondering how long it would be before she stopped shaking.

She felt like that silly cartoon character who kept getting steamrollered flat as a pancake, only to pop back up and get knocked flat again.

Except she didn't know how many more hits she could take and still get back up again.

How many surprises did he have left for her? she wondered.

"Rebecca?"

She looked up to find Brian in the doorway.

"He told you, didn't he?"

"Yes."

Brian came in and closed the door. "Let me—"

Rebecca slapped him on the cheek, surprising him at least as much as she surprised herself. Horrified herself, actually.

"I'm sorry," she said.

"I'm sorry, too."

"I mean about everything."

"Me, too."

Rebecca looked at him, looked hard and wondered why she couldn't have just loved him, why she couldn't have married him years ago and been happy with him.

"I wish—"

"There's nothing left to say, Brian."

He nodded slowly, and he didn't try to stop her when she walked out the door.

Chapter 17

Rebecca paused after closing the front door to her parents' house and looked over at the garage to the apartment where Tucker was staying.

She'd brooded all night, then shortly after nine decided that she wanted to talk to Tucker. So she'd bundled up a sleepy Sammy and taken him to her parents' to spend the night.

Now that she was here, she could tell that his car was missing and no lights were on at the apartment.

She walked around the house to the patio, then out among the roses in the garden, the last ones of the season now in full bloom.

Rebecca bent over one peach-colored bloom and inhaled deeply, remembering the scent, remembering the day when Brian had returned home to find her married, pregnant and miserable with her husband.

She looked back toward the house to the darkened windows and doors and wondered where Tucker had been standing when he'd heard Brian say that he loved her and wanted her back.

And she wondered what she would have done if Tucker had simply asked her what she wanted to do. If he had offered her a choice—him or Brian—instead of making that choice for her.

She wasn't sure about then, but now, knowing what she did after years spent trying to be happy with Brian, she knew what she would have done.

She would have stayed with her husband. Maybe they would have made it, and maybe they wouldn't have. If they hadn't, it wouldn't have been all Tucker's fault. Rebecca had been so young, so insecure, so jealous, so overwhelmed by her powerful, self-assured husband.

Most of all, she'd never felt quite secure in his love, never understood why he'd chosen her, and always wondered when he'd see for himself that he'd made a mistake in doing so.

So she hadn't been very surprised to find him with Cheryl Atkinson that day. It had confirmed every insecurity she'd ever had.

Rebecca shook her head as if to clear it of the memories. She looked up at the moon, at the starlit sky, and told herself once and for all that it was time to look ahead and not behind her.

She wasn't that young, insecure girl anymore.

And Tucker wasn't the same man, either. She believed that.

She'd gone back into the commission's chambers and watched him arguing his case before them. He was so calm, so self-assured, so passionate about it all.

And she'd been proud of him and of the work he was doing. She'd never felt that before about his work.

And she loved watching him with Sammy. They were still a little unsure of each other, still a little wary, but there was a bond there. There was love between them, and it grew stronger every day.

Rebecca wondered now, if...

She turned at the sound of a car driving up and got a funny, fluttery feeling in her chest.

The door slammed, then footsteps sounded on the driveway and the steps leading up to Tucker's apartment.

Time to face him.

Time to face up to her feelings and decide what she was going to do.

Tucker was taking off his tie and unbuttoning his shirt when he heard a knock at the door.

"Rebecca?" He went still for a minute when he saw her. He would swear that his heart lurched to a halt, then started pounding twice as fast as it should.

He turned away, left her there in the open door, because he was aching to touch her, aching to pull her close and tell her that he loved her one more time.

What if he never got to do that again?

This afternoon—that whole scene had shaken him badly, and he knew it had shaken her. He had a feeling he was about to find out how much.

"Come on in," he said over his shoulder. "I thought that was your car in the driveway. Everything all right with your parents?"

"Yes," she said softly. "I left Sammy over there because I wanted to talk to you."

His heart stopped again. He couldn't bring himself to look at her because he could always see so much of what was in her heart in the expression on her face.

And he was scared of what was in her heart.

Tucker closed his eyes and shoved his hands into his pockets. God, he wanted this woman back.

"Rebecca, I'm sorry about that scene at the office today. I wish I'd told you the whole thing sooner, but ... I just wanted some time. I wanted us to have some time together...." He waited, knowing that whatever came out of their conversation tonight would mean the world to him.

She meant the world to him.

"I wish you'd told me six years ago," she said.

He turned to face her at that, seeing less of her feelings than he expected in her big green eyes. Or maybe she was getting better at hiding them from him.

"So do I," he said.

She walked a little further inside the room, crowded now, even with the little bit of furniture he'd brought.

He didn't care. He hadn't expected to spend that much time here.

He'd hoped. God, he'd hoped that before too long he and Rebecca and Sammy would be finding their own house to share.

He wondered now if they ever would.

"I've been wondering," she said, "what I would have done if you had given me a choice."

Him or Brian the wonder boy?

Tucker had never felt he could have given her a choice. What if they had stayed together? What if they'd made Sammy as miserable as his parents had made him?

She came a little closer, and he was glad he had his hands in his pockets, because he wanted, so much, to reach out and grab her, to hold her to him and never let her go.

"I think," she said, "I don't know what I would have decided."

Tucker pulled on one end of his already-loosened tie until it was free of his collar, then walked to the door of the bedroom and threw it inside on top of the bureau.

He thought about going into the bedroom, putting some distance between her and him, but—

The phone rang, and he looked at his watch and wondered if everything could have come together this fast.

"I'm sorry," he said. "I've been working on this all night, and something may have broken."

He picked up the phone by the bedside table. It was Bill Marshall, the attorney for the paper mill company. He'd talked to the owners, and they'd agreed to consider abandoning their project in favor of selling the land to the county or the state fast—whoever could come up with the money.

Tucker had just found out this afternoon that the company was having some financial problems, that its expansion plans were in jeopardy because of them. He hadn't even had time to talk with the commission chairman about it before the meeting, so he'd had to surprise everyone by delaying the scheduled hearing on the appeal.

Now he'd spent all night working on a plan for the county or the state to buy the paper mill property back.

And he'd won—if he could just find some agency with some money to spend ... or if he could get Rebecca to raise a few million dollars for him.

"Thanks, Bill," he said into the phone. "I'll call you first thing in the morning as soon as we can get everybody together."

He stared at the wall in front of him and wanted to tell her, wanted to share this with her. But he didn't, because there would be no victory if he lost her for good. And that was what he was facing tonight.

"Is everything all right?" She came up behind him, and he froze there, looking at the bed.

He'd been so hopeful that night he'd spent in her bed. And he hadn't slept since that night. He'd just lain in the bed and relived that night, then thought about all he wanted to share with her in the future.

"Yeah. Things are fine. Tell me about you and Brian."

She put her hand on his arm, surprising him. "Tucker, it would have been a mistake for me to be with Brian. I know that now."

He didn't say anything. He couldn't.

"Ask me why," she said.

He turned to face her.

She surprised him again by putting her palms flat against his chest. One thumb slipped in between the ends of the shirt that no longer met and rubbed up and down, so slowly.

"Why?" he asked, his voice as rough as gravel.

She stood there with one of her palms over his heart, his runaway heart.

"Because I never loved him the way I loved you."

Loved, he told himself before he could get too hopeful. She said loved. Not love.

"I tried to make it work for the longest time, but it just didn't. And I thought for a while it was me—that something was wrong with me, but it wasn't. It was Brian and me—we just weren't right together."

Tucker couldn't stand it anymore. He took her by the shoulders and held her there, where she was, about six inches from his chest.

He didn't want her to get any further than that but was afraid to pull her any closer.

"What about now, Rebecca? What about us?"

She hesitated. It seemed to go on forever, and the whole time he was easing her closer, all the time surprised that she didn't protest.

He let himself kiss her once, softly, then again, like a starving man come face-to-face with a king's feast.

"I still love you, Rebecca," he said against her lips, then kissed her some more.

He tasted her again and again, wondering how he'd managed to go so long without the taste of her lips on his, wondering how he'd ever manage again.

"Rebecca. Tell me something."

She eased away from him, and he stopped her when she would have gotten too far away.

"I'm not ready for that, Tucker. I can't tell you that I love you yet."

He looked away at that and wondered if he'd have to literally pry his hands off her upper arms.

God, he was going to have to let her go.

"But," she said, tilting his head back toward her so she could look at him, so he had no choice but to look at her, "but I want to try."

Tucker almost fell to the floor.

She smiled at him, and he was surprised he was still standing.

"We have to be careful, for Sammy. I don't want him to get hurt."

"He won't be," he said, still in a daze.

"And we have to go slowly. It's going to take some time."

He smiled down at her as tears filled her eyes and a single one rolled down her cheek.

"You've got it," he said. "As much as you need."

"And I'm still scared, but it doesn't seem to matter that much anymore. I just . . . I still feel like I belong to you, like we belong together."

"We do."

Another tear fell down her cheek, and he wiped it away for her.

"I've missed you, Tucker."

He groaned and settled her body intimately against his. "I thought I was going to die without you."

She pulled his mouth down to hers and kissed him the way she had that night, when they'd spent all night loving each other.

"Rebecca," he said as they both came up for air. "How would you feel about coming to bed with me?"

She gave him a sinfully beautiful smile.

"We could go slowly," he offered. "Take as much time as you need."

He'd been backing her up until the bed was against her legs. And then she let herself go limp in his arms, catching him off guard, throwing him off balance.

Together, with laughter and tears of joy, they fell onto the bed.

Epilogue

It was almost Christmas, and Sammy was excited.

He ran ahead of his mom and dad into the store to look at all the pretty lights on all the trees.

"Hey, look at that one! Look how big it is!"

Sammy looked way up at the tall tree, and when his parents didn't answer, he turned around to see what was going on.

They were kissing again and doing all that mushy stuff.

Sammy started to yell at them again, but didn't.

He just didn't understand.

Jimmy Horton said kissing was gross.

But then, Jimmy didn't believe in birthday wishes coming true or in Santa Claus, either. Sammy wasn't worried about that, 'cause his dad said Jimmy Horton didn't know everything, 'cause he was only seven years old.

B'sides, Sammy knew birthday wishes came true, because he'd wished his dad back.

Sammy turned around again, now that he was tired of waiting.

"Come on, you guys. We have to find Santa."

They'd almost caught up with him when Sammy ran on ahead. He had to talk to Santa, 'cause he had an extra-special wish he had to make, and it was almost Christmas.

They finally found Santa in the store, 'n' they had to wait in a big, long line till it was Sammy's turn.

Sammy finally climbed up on Santa's lap, and he wasn't scared. Not a bit.

Santa made him laugh and let him pull his whiskers to show that they really were real, 'n' then he asked what Sammy wanted for Christmas.

Sammy tugged on the whiskers again until Santa leaned down so that Sammy could whisper it to him, 'cause everybody knew wishes had to be secrets if they were going to come true.

He told Santa that he wanted his dad to come home and live with him and his mom, forever and ever.

Santa looked down at the serious-minded little boy, then turned to look at his parents, standing close together, at ease that way, the handsome, smiling man with his arm around the pretty woman.

Santa always got a lot of Christmas wishes that he knew he couldn't make come true all on his own, and this was always the hardest one.

He didn't like to make promises he couldn't keep, but Santa believed in miracles, especially Christmas miracles. And he liked to make the little children happy.

"Can you do it, Santa?" Sammy asked.

Santa looked at the man and the woman again, looked deep into their hearts—Santa could do that—and figured it was a pretty safe promise to make to a good little boy like Sammy.

Santa patted Sammy on the back and winked at him with a twinkle in his eye and gave him a big "Ho, ho, ho!"

"I think I can, Sammy."

*   *   *   *   *

by Linda Turner

Out in The Wild West, life is rough, tough and dangerous, but the Rawlings family can handle anything that comes their way—well, *almost* anything!

American Hero Cooper Rawlings didn't know what hit him when he met Susannah Patterson, daughter of the man who'd shot his brother in the back. He *should* have hated her on sight. But he didn't. Instead he found himself saddling up and riding to her rescue when someone began sabotaging her ranch and threatening her life. Suddenly lassoing this beautiful but stubborn little lady into his arms was the only thing he could think about.

Don't miss COOPER (IM #553), available in March. And look for the rest of the clan's stories—Flynn and Kat's—as Linda Turner's exciting saga continues in

THE WILD WEST

Coming to you throughout 1994...only from Silhouette Intimate Moments.

Take 4 bestselling love stories FREE

Plus get a FREE surprise gift!

Special Limited-time Offer

Mail to Silhouette Reader Service™

3010 Walden Avenue
P.O. Box 1867
Buffalo, N.Y. 14269-1867

YES! Please send me 4 free Silhouette Intimate Moments® novels and my free surprise gift. Then send me 6 brand-new novels every month, which I will receive months before they appear in bookstores. Bill me at the low price of $2.89 each plus 25¢ delivery and applicable sales tax, if any.* That's the complete price and—compared to the cover prices of $3.50 each—quite a bargain! I understand that accepting the books and gift places me under no obligation ever to buy any books. I can always return a shipment and cancel at any time. Even if I never buy another book from Silhouette, the 4 free books and the surprise gift are mine to keep forever.

245 BPA ANRR

Name	(PLEASE PRINT)	
Address	Apt. No.	
City	State	Zip

This offer is limited to one order per household and not valid to present Silhouette Intimate Moments® subscribers. *Terms and prices are subject to change without notice. Sales tax applicable in N.Y.

UMOM-94R   ©1990 Harlequin Enterprises Limited

HE'S AN

AMERICAN HERO

January 1994 rings in the New Year—and a new lineup of sensational American Heroes. You can't seem to get enough of these men, and we're proud to feature one each month, created by some of your favorite authors.

January: CUTS BOTH WAYS by Dee Holmes: Erin Kenyon hired old acquaintance Ashe Seager to investigate the crash that claimed her husband's life, only to learn old memories never die.

February: A WANTED MAN by Kathleen Creighton: Mike Lanagan's exposé on corruption earned him accolades...and the threat of death. Running for his life, he found sanctuary in the arms of Lucy Brown—but for how long?

March: COOPER by Linda Turner: Cooper Rawlings wanted nothing to do with the daughter of the man who'd shot his brother. But when someone threatened Susannah Patterson's life, he found himself riding to the rescue....

AMERICAN HEROES: Men who give all they've got for their country, their work—the women they love.

Only from

It's our 1000th
Silhouette Romance
and we're celebrating!

Join us for a special collection of love stories by the authors you've loved for years, and new favorites you've just discovered.

It's a celebration just for you,
with wonderful books by
Diana Palmer, Suzanne Carey,
Tracy Sinclair, Marie Ferrarella,
Debbie Macomber, Laurie Paige,
Annette Broadrick, Elizabeth August
and MORE!

Silhouette Romance...vibrant, fun and emotionally rich! Take another look at us!

As part of the celebration, readers can receive a FREE gift AND enter our exciting sweepstakes to win a grand prize of $1000! Look for more details in all March Silhouette series titles.

You'll fall in love all over again
with Silhouette Romance!

As seen on TV!

Free Gift Offer

With a Free Gift proof-of-purchase from any Silhouette® book,
you can receive a beautiful cubic zirconia pendant.

This gorgeous marquise-shaped stone is a genuine cubic
zirconia—accented by an 18" gold tone necklace.

(Approximate retail value $19.95)

Send for yours today...

compliments of ▼ *Silhouette*®

To receive your free gift, a cubic zirconia pendant, send us one original proof-of-
purchase, photocopies not accepted, from the back of any Silhouette Romance™,
Silhouette Desire®, Silhouette Special Edition®, Silhouette Intimate Moments® or
Silhouette Shadows™ title for January, February or March 1994 at your favorite retail
outlet, together with the Free Gift Certificate, plus a check or money order for $2.50
(do not send cash) to cover postage and handling, payable to Silhouette Free Gift Offer.
We will send you the specified gift. Allow 6 to 8 weeks for delivery. Offer good until
March 31st, 1994 or while quantities last. Offer valid in the U.S. and Canada only.

Free Gift Certificate

Name: _____

Address: _____

City: _____ State/Province: _____ Zip/Postal Code: _____

Mail this certificate, one proof-of-purchase and a check or money order for postage
and handling to: SILHOUETTE FREE GIFT OFFER 1994. In the U.S.: 3010 Walden
Avenue, P.O. Box 9057, Buffalo NY 14269-9057. In Canada: P.O. Box 622, Fort Erie,
Ontario L2Z 5X3

FREE GIFT OFFER   079-KBZ
ONE PROOF-OF-PURCHASE
To collect your fabulous FREE GIFT, a cubic zirconia pendant, you must include this
original proof-of-purchase for each gift with the properly completed Free Gift Certificate.

079-KBZ